wonderland

wonderland

Joanna Nadin

CANDLEWICK PRESS

Copyright © 2009 by Joanna Nadin

First U.S. edition 2011

Library of Congress Cataloging-in-Publication Data is available.

Library of Congress Catalog Card Number 2010038715

ISBN 978-0-7636-4846-6

10 11 12 13 14 15 BVG 10 9 8 7 6 5 4 3 2 1

Printed in Berryville, VA, U.S.A.

This book was typeset in Fairfield LH.

Candlewick Press
99 Dover Street
Somerville, Massachusetts 02144

visit us at www.candlewick.com

For those of us who have lived in the shadow of others

With thanks to Averil Whitehouse, without whom this book would never have come into the light

prologue

August

BE YOURSELF, they say. Be whoever you want to be. Dad, Ed, Mr. Hughes, Oprah bloody Winfrey. Like some crappy mantra.

But they're not the same thing. Not the same thing at all.

I look at my reflection in the rearview mirror. My hair bottle-bleached and salt-dirty, my eyes ringed in black, lips stained red. My hands on the steering wheel, knuckles white, the nail varnish chipped, weeks old. Then I look at the Point, falling away in front of us. The wooden fence, broken from where we've climbed over it so many times. The ledge below, cigarette-strewn and soaked in lager. And the sea below that. A swirling, monstrous, beautiful thing. Alive.

Nausea rises in me again, bubbling up, insistent. I breathe in, pushing it, willing it back down again. I don't know how we got here. How I got here. I don't mean how I got to this place, the Point, but how I became the girl in the mirror. I don't recognize myself. What I look like. What I'm doing.

I used to know who I was. Jude. Named after a song in the hope that I'd stand out and shine. But I didn't. Jude the Invisible. Jude the Obscure. Everything about me unremarkable. Nothing beautiful or striking, to make people say, "You know, the girl with that hair," or those eyes. I was just the girl from the farm. The one with no mum. I knew what would happen when I woke up, when I went to school, when I came home. Who would talk to me. Who wouldn't.

Until Stella. Now when I look in the mirror, I see someone else staring back. I can't see where I stop and Stella begins.

"We'll be legend," I say.

I watch Stella as she lights up a cigarette and drops the Zippo on the dash.

"Like Thelma and Louise," she drawls. She takes a drag, then passes it to me. "But without the head scarves or Brad Pitt or the heart-of-gold cop watching us die."

And then I know she knows. And I know she won't stop me. Because this is the only way.

"It'll be very," she says.

I take a long drag on the cigarette and, still watching myself in the mirror, exhale slowly. *Shouldn't be smoking,* I think. But what difference does it make now? I pass it back to Stella. Then I let the hand brake off and the car rolls forward.

I

May

I'M SITTING in my bedroom, looking in the mirror. Her mirror. The wood scratched, glass flyblown. In front of it, a bottle of Chanel No. 5, the perfume evaporated to a dark amber, the label yellowed, peeling now. I hear Dad and Alfie downstairs, clattering in the kitchen. Alfie asking for Coco Pops and Dad saying no. Like it's any other morning. But it's not.

I'm wondering what she'd look like today. Her thirty-sixth birthday. I think of Ed's mum, Mrs. Hickman. Working in the post office with Dad. Her hair graying, clothes shapeless, in every shade of beige. Or Mrs. Applegate. Red-faced, rolls of fat bulging under her rugby top. Soft-focus, blurry versions of who they once were. But Mum never changes. Twenty-eight forever. Model looks, she still went up to London for shoots. But it's here I picture her. Sundress hitched up around her legs, hair this wild gold, curls whipping around her shoulders in the sea wind, the silver of her hooped earrings catching in the sunlight. Laughing as we rolled down the dunes, sand in our eyes and shoes and knickers. She shone. Bright and sure. Even at the end. She still eclipsed us all.

They say I look like her. Gran, Mrs. Hickman, even that woman in the pub. I remember she was watching the deliverymen roll the beer barrels off the lorry. My hand felt small in Dad's rough heavy grip as he pulled me up the hill toward home. I held him back, straining to peer into the cellar, wondering what ghosts and creatures hid there in the damp darkness. I felt the words almost before I heard them. Shooting through him, his hand stiffening on mine. "Hasn't she got Charlie's eyes?"

She meant nothing. Trying to be nice. Or just remembering. But he didn't want to remember. He pulled me away up the hill. Me apologizing for her. "Sorry, Dad." Like I could make her take the words back. Make them evaporate. And take the memory with them.

I know he sees her when he looks at me. Sees that day. Me jumping up and down on the bed like it's a trampoline, shouting at her, "Get up, get up, get up!" Her lying on her side. Saying she just needs another hour. Dad dragging me off, telling me to leave her alone. That she's too tired. That we're wearing her out, me and Alfie.

That was the last time I saw her.

I look at my reflection again, turn my head. Trying to see what they see: her eyes, her smile. But it's just me. Brown eyes. Straight hair, a nothing color. Nose too big. I am the blurry one. The faded version.

I know why she did it. It wasn't me. Not just me, anyway. It was this place. The people. All of it. She thought it would be her escape. Her wilderness. Her Happy Valley. But it suffocated her. And I can feel it taking me too. The memory of her weighs down on me, squeezing the breath out of my lungs. I gasp and brace myself against the dresser. My right hand slips on something. I look down, and the weight lifts. I pick the envelope up and read the address again. My handwriting, deliberate, practiced. Like my letters to Santa Claus when I was six years old. It cannot get lost; its contents are too precious. Inside is my golden ticket. My escape from this life. An application form for drama school three hundred miles away in London. Because there I might shine. There I can be somebody else.

Then I see it. A flash of green flickering across the mirror. I look up and she is standing there. Back against the wall, hair pinned up. Her dress a shiny emerald, like the carapace of a beetle. She smiles. And though I know what will happen, what always happens, I turn. And she is gone. And I hear Dad shout up the stairs. "Jude. Bus. Now."

I pick the envelope up off the dresser and put it in my bag, hiding it among the books. I'll post it later, I think. In town. Not here. Someone will see it. He'll see it. Recognize the writing. Nothing stays secret for long in a place like this.

But as I walk down the stairs, my school shoes clopping on the bare boards, I can feel the letter burning, screaming its presence. Like she did. Like I wish I could. And I wonder if today I'll dare to post it. Or if I'll bury it at the bottom of my drawer again. Lost for another month under my primary-school coloring books and swimming certificates. And I know the answer. And I hate myself.

2

THE BUS takes half an hour to make the six miles from Churchtown to Porth. I sit alone at the back, slumped against the window in the dull, heavy heat as we trail a tractor out of the village. Listening to the tinny chat of the driver's radio crackle into our world, out of place against the high-hedged lanes. The DJ talking about his night out in London, about places and people three hundred miles away. About a rush hour that doesn't move. Cabs and cars jammed into the buzzing streets.

We pull out onto the roundabout and join the pitiful queue of cars making their way toward the few chain shops and offices that pass for a town. And I listen to the radio and wish I were in that world, not this.

Royal Duchy Girls' School is where weekenders and rich locals send their kids, thinking it's going to be all Enid Blyton with sea air, outdoor pursuits, and bread and jam for tea. What it doesn't say in the glossy prospectus is that outdoor pursuits means burying bottles of vodka in the dunes to dig up later or shagging sixth-formers from County Boys' on the hockey pitch. Or that, forget bread and jam, the upper-school dorms are redolent with the acid waft of bulimic vomit—this year's bikini diet of choice—and that half of Year Eleven are regularly in the Priory for rehab. I loathe school. And it loathes me. Four hundred overachievers, toxic anorexics, and It Girl wannabes, all crammed into a Victorian Gothic horror house on a hill.

And as if that weren't bad enough, there's Emily Applegate. My own personal rich-kid nightmare. If you just heard her name, you'd think she was all rosy cheeks and white lace, like some Jane Austen heroine, or a nice-as-pie vicar's daughter. She's not. She's a grade-A bitch who only exists to torment and torture lesser beings. Like me. And, like every supervillain, she has minions. Three of them. The Plastics, Ed calls them. Holly Scott, Holly Harker, and Claudia Dawson. Dawce. All blond hair and trust funds and weekend coke habits.

And just my luck. They all do drama.

It's the last lesson before exams. Before review sessions and Brodie's Notes and late-night panic attacks and Prozac on prescription. But not me. I won't. I can't. I don't even drink. Not seriously, anyway. Because I don't want to be like him. He thinks I don't know, but I've seen the bottle. Everything's fine, he says. But it's not. It never is.

So we're sitting in the theater. It's dark and cool, the hazy heat of the school and town shut out. The only sound is Holly Harker's laughter echoing off the walls as she recounts last night's trash TV.

This is my world, my private kingdom. Has been ever since Mum took me to Drury Lane when I was six, to see some old friend of hers play Fagin in *Oliver*. "It's hardly the Royal National Theatre," she said. "But you'll love it anyway." And she was right. I was hooked. As the lights dimmed and the first notes of the overture played out across the rows of plush red seats, I could barely breathe. And as the curtain went up to reveal the perfectly rendered filth of the workhouse, I knew what I wanted to do and where I wanted to be.

I begged her to take me again. If not to London, to Plymouth. Dad would say we needed the money for salt blocks or fencing, but she always found a way. It was our drug. It still is mine. Pulling me in with its gaudy lights and greasepaint and promise of something more, something better. Under the lights, when the faces of the crowd are just an inky swirl in the distance. This is where I can be someone else. Where I can be who I want to be.

But for now I'm sitting at the side, in the shadows. Making myself invisible. Listening to Mr. Hughes — Hughsie — telling us that acting's not the easy option. That we need to work hard. That we won't just walk out of the Duchy gates and onto the set of *Hollyoaks*.

"It's a slog. It takes courage. And wit. And hard bloody work." He pauses between each word. Taking pleasure in them. In their sound. And their effect. I watch Emily look up from her nails. Hear some of the others snigger. Thrilled at him swearing. Breaking the rules.

"And one of you is making it even tougher for herself."

The laughter falls away into silence. Holly Harker flicks a glance across at Emily, wondering if they were seen up at the Point two weeks ago, drinking when they were supposed to be in rehearsal. But it's not that. No one is in trouble. Instead he turns to me. And I know what he's going to say and my stomach rises into my throat. And I'm thinking, *Don't say it, don't say it, don't say it.* Willing him to stop. But he doesn't.

"Jude Polmear has applied to the Lab in London. And I think she has a serious chance of getting in. So, before we go, let's wish her luck."

My face is burning red, my head down, staring at a scuff mark on the floor. But I can still see their faces, lit with scorn and delight at finding the secret I've been carrying. And what they can do with it.

It was his idea. Mr. Hughes's. I needed his reference to apply. But I wish I hadn't listened to him, to his belief in me. Because his voice is drowned out now by their mocking and my own self-doubt.

11

Emily corners me at the lockers, the Plastics behind her, blocking my exit. "Who do you think you are? Keira Knightley?"

"Shut up, Emily." But it's not an order. It's pathetic. Pleading.

She slams my locker door shut and grabs the key, forcing me to face her.

"Give it back. . . ." But it's a whisper.

She mimics Mr. Hughes: "Project, Polmear. I can't hear you."

Dawce laughs.

"Give it back," I plead. Louder this time.

"I can't hear you."

Tears prick the backs of my eyes. Too near the surface. Like hers. Mum's. Just waiting to come out. "Give it back!" I yell. People stop in the corridor, staring and whispering behind their hands.

Emily laughs.

"Please . . ." A tear escapes, running down my cheek. I wipe it away. "Please," I whisper again.

She drops my key on the floor. I stoop to pick it up, and the heel of her shoe crunches on my hand as she walks away.

I stand at the school gates, on my way to the bus. I can see the postbox ahead, its gaping jaw waiting, black against the red. But Emily is right. Who do I think I am? I walk past without stopping.

3

I WASN'T always like this. Diminished. A shadow. Once I was as bright as she was. People took notice, because she was with me. Stella.

She came when I was eight. Just showed up at school one day, chewing Doublemint gum, and sat at the desk next to mine. The desk that had been empty ever since Dawce had begged to be moved, complaining that I muttered and talked to myself. But Stella didn't care what I did. I was her best friend. And she was mine.

Her hair was blond, hanging down her back, and wild, like her eyes. She didn't care what anyone thought. Even then. The world turned for her alone.

It was Stella who taught me to swear. "Shit bloody

piss." As soon as I said the words, I willed them to disappear. But, defiant, they hung in the air between me and Dad. Still there, after he'd sent me to my room. Still there during tea, their rounded shapes appearing in the Alphabetti Spaghetti. I never swore at him again. But that second of pleasure stayed with me. Even after Stella left.

Now I sometimes wonder if she was real. If she actually existed. No one mentions her name. She's been erased. Like Mum.

But she did exist.

I find it when I'm pushing the letter back down to the bottom of my drawer. I see the childish loops of my first ink pen, of the eight-year-old me, peering out from the shelter of an old birthday card. I pull it out, carefully. Like it might bite. Or burn. Like it's dangerous. Because that's what she was, Stella. Dangerous. And then I read.

When I Grow Up
by Jude Polmear, Year Three

When I grow up, I want to be my friend Stella. I met her one week and three days after my mum went to heaven, which is where you can eat what you like even Mars bars all day and no one says your teeth will fall out. My mum was called Charlotte Emma Polmear and she wore pink shoes and once she kissed a pop star. But this isn't about my mum—it's about

Stella. Stella is eight years old, the same as me, and six centimeters taller. She wears makeup and her mum's clothes and is allowed to drink Slush Puppies and watch grown-up films at the same time. I am allowed to drink Slush Puppies, but only on weekends and never if Gran is here. The best thing about Stella is that she isn't afraid of dares. Sometimes her dares are bad, like when she dared me to cut off Emily Applegate's ponytail. I said I was sorry about it a million times and anyway her hair is still longer than mine. Stella has blond hair and it is wavy. My hair is straight and brown but it is shiny when you put conditioner in it. My dad says Stella is a bad influence, which means she makes me do bad things when really I am good, but I don't think she means to. It is just that her rules are different. We have a lot of rules in our house. Like no elbows on the table and no wearing school shoes in the cowshed and especially no letting Alfie in with the cows on his own. Alfie is my brother. He is not even in school yet. Stella doesn't have any brothers or sisters. She is an only child, which means she does not have to share anything ever and she gets to call her mum and dad Georgie and Jack. When we grow up, me and Stella are going to live in the same house and eat chips and strawberry mousse every day and we will be actresses or on the Olympic team for gymnastics. So that is who I would like to be. Stella says you can be anyone you want. She read it in a book.

I lie back on the bed and close my eyes, the memory coursing through my blood, a dangerous heat. And I wish. I wish that Stella would come back. Because then I could post the letter. Then I could be someone else again. Someone who swears. And dares. And shines.

4

June

I STOPPED believing in fairy godmothers a long time ago, along with Santa Claus and good triumphing over evil. But somehow, someone grants my wish. Because three weeks later she's back.

The GCSE French exam is over, and I'm in the dunes, doing handstands like some schoolkid. I am some schoolkid. For now—my kilt hanging upside down, hem falling around my chest, regulation knickers up to my waist. Looking at the new world order, sky at the bottom, sea and beach at the top. That's when I see her. Taller now. Ray-Bans on, the black lace of her bra showing. Packet of cigarettes in her hand. Stella.

"Jesus, Jude, those knickers are huge. Where'd you get them? Your gran?"

"Stella . . . ?" My arms buckle and I fall gracelessly into the sand. My heart races and I think I'm going to be sick. With happiness. Or fear. Then I think maybe it's not her. That I've imagined her. That when I turn, she'll be gone. Like in the mirror.

But when I look, she's still there. Beautiful and bright like she always was.

"What are you doing that for, anyway?" She folds her arms and looks down at me. "Handstands are for five-year-olds."

"Oh, my God, Stella . . . what are you doing here?"

"Nice to see you too." She sits down next to me. "Dad's painting here for the summer. Got an exhibition next month. I'm helping him."

I wonder about school. If she's been expelled. Finally. "Haven't you got exams?"

"Done them."

I wait for her to say something else. Like which ones, or how they were. But Stella never went in for details. Or tests. Said life wasn't about what grade you got. Said half of Hollywood never even went to school. And I think of her working with her dad. His model. His inspiration. "His Muse," I say.

Stella looks out to sea. "Something like that." She taps the cigarette packet hard on the sand. Packing the tobacco down. A pro. Like Ed's mates up at the Point. Learning tricks with their lighters. Blowing smoke rings.

She peels off the cellophane, letting it catch the wind, the sun glinting off its transparency as it disappears into the heat and light. I watch her, fascinated, as she flicks the packet and a single cigarette shoots up. She takes it with her lips, gloss staining the paper. Pulls out a brass Zippo. Something engraved on it. Her name, I think. Or a boy's. Then she lights it, shielding it from the wind, hair whipping around her face, and the smell of lighter fluid in the air. I will learn to love that smell.

"Want one?"

I shake my head. Then regret it. I should have taken one. Everyone around here smokes. At school it's practically compulsory.

Stella shrugs and lies back on the sand. "I called for you at the post office, but an alligator told me you'd be down here."

"Crocodile," I say. "Alfie." My little brother. Nine and still obsessed with dressing up. Yesterday he was Spider-Man. Teachers have given up on sending him home.

"He's grown. Anyway, what's the difference?"

"Um. Head shape, apparently." I fidget, not sure whether to lie down too. I try stretching my legs out but it feels odd. Instead, I pull my skirt over my knees and clutch them tight. "So, how'd you know to try the post office?"

"God's sake, Jude." Stella lifts her sunglasses up and

looks at me. "This is Churchtown, not Los Angeles. You can't cough without someone knowing. Your dad's glittering career change is headline news." She lets the glasses drop again.

I feel heat surge to my cheeks. The last time Stella was here, we lived at the farm. The farm Dad swore he would never take over, but did anyway when his father died. The farm he left London for, bringing his pregnant girlfriend with him, happy to follow, saying it would be an adventure. Dad said she'd read too many daft books, that she was living in a dream world, but she came anyway, head full of the romance of *Rebecca* and bleak moors and wave-battered beaches. But there's no romance in farming. In the mud and the rain and the bellowing of sick cows and the getting up at dawn.

The farm that sent her quietly mad and then drove her away for good. The farm he clung on to through foot-and-mouth, only to lose it a year later. Subsidies forcing him to pour good milk down the drain. Supermarkets cutting prices. Had enough, he said. Can't fight it anymore. Without her, is what he meant. So the farm got sold off for holiday cottages, and I could feel the village's silent pity bearing down on us. Lost their mum; now lost their home. Until he bought the old post office/general store and was reborn as some kind of local hero. Nothing heroic in stacking shelves, though. Still has to get up at dawn.

"So, what is with the underwear?" says Stella, stubbing her cigarette out in the sand. "And that skirt. It's hideous."

I come to. "Oh. Royal Duchy. . . . Bad, huh?"

She lets out a short, harsh laugh. "Jesus. Who's paying for that? Your gran?"

I say nothing. But Stella knows she's right. It's Gran's compromise for the boarding school she really wanted me to go to. Mum's old school. Some redbrick building in Surrey with stables and a lacrosse team and a foreign secretary in the alumni. Dad stood his ground for months for the local high school, but in the end he said he couldn't be bothered to argue anymore. Another battle conceded.

"Bloody bookworm. Bet you love it." Stella stands up, the sun making a halo behind her. Like an angel. Wearing Topshop and Rimmel. "So, can I come over later, or have you got Latin review or something?"

"No . . . uh, I mean, yeah. Sure." I am not sure at all. But I don't know what else to say. And anyway, Stella doesn't take no for an answer.

"Great. Later, then. It'll be very."

"Very what?"

"Very. Just very . . . Remember?"

And I do remember. A movie. *Heathers*. Stella spoke in film lines. She said it made her sound interesting. Compared to most people around here, I guess it did.

She turns to walk up the cliff path. I call after her. "Where are you staying?"

She looks over her shoulder. "At the farm."

"Oh," I say, shocked, unable to keep the pointless exclamation from bursting out. But she doesn't notice. Or says nothing.

21

"In the old milking shed. 'Seaview,' it's called now. That's a joke. Can't even see the Point."

She smiles. And then I smile. And she is gone.

Self-consciousness gone with her, I fall back on the sand, sun burning down on me. I can hear each breath, each heartbeat a thud-thud against the sea. She's back. I try to remember what she looked like when I saw her last. And I realize I can't remember her leaving. The last time, I mean. She just stopped coming around. Then one day I went to find her at the cottage, and it was empty, the door left ajar. Nothing inside but a few crisp packets and a Barbie strung above the door in mock suicide. My Barbie. The one I'd begged for months for. That Dad had refused to get me, so I sobbed to Gran and it arrived the next week. Pink and glittery and perfect. For a month she'd stayed in her box, away from Alfie's sticky fingers, only coming out for a few minutes each day. Until Stella decided she needed a makeover. So we cut her hair and dyed it black with the ink from Dad's cartridge pen. Totally Winona, Stella had said, and hung her up like Lydia in *Beetlejuice,* a film I'd seen once when Dad was away. Mum and me curled up on the sofa with popcorn and Pepsi and old videos. Films that were packed away in cardboard boxes and stashed in the attic when she died.

I thought I'd seen Stella a few times since then. Usually out on the Point, where we used to hide when she was in trouble. Which was a lot. And once in town, when I'd bunked off PE to meet Ed at HMV, heart pounding in case one of the teachers was on a break and caught me.

But, when I looked properly, it was never really her. Just some girl with blond hair and an attitude. Or nobody at all.

And I thought about her, on and off. When I was in a handstand, mostly. Like at primary school. "Handstand Wonderland" it was called. And Stella excelled at it. Her legs poker straight in the hazy sunshine, then falling apart into splits and scissors. The Year Six boys lined up on the bank watching, waiting for a glimpse of what was underneath her dress.

That's when I first saw what her confidence could buy. Drinking pink milk at break and watching Emily Applegate's lot doing handstands, upside down in a row, waving their legs in a jelly wobble. I just watched. I didn't play. Not with them, anyway. Didn't dare. But Stella just walks up and says, "I'm in."

Emily, upright now, looks her up and down like she is some kind of alien being. Which she is, kind of. "You can't just join in. You've got to be invited."

"Yeah?"

Then she does a perfect Long John Silver, one leg crooked up, for a whole minute, and everyone, even Emily, is in silent reverence. A new queen is crowned. And, reluctantly, I am allowed in with her. Practicing in the dunes after school, the soft sand breaking our fall. Or up against the cowshed walls, our sandals scuffing on the rough wood.

And I never stopped after that. Not when Stella left. Or when Emily and the others moved on to chase-and-kiss, then smoking in the bus shelter. I carried on. Because I could. And I was good at it. And everything looks different that way up. More interesting.

When I wake up, it's late. My face is sore from the afternoon sun, my legs leaden, drugged with sleep. But then my stomach flips. With what? Guilt, maybe. I should be studying, not playing in the sand like a kid. But it's not that. Exams are over now, but for one. The long days and late nights shut in my room, in my head, trying to burn chemistry and math and which king killed who and when into my memory. It's done.

Then I remember. And I can feel it build inside me. Not guilt. Anticipation.

Red fireworks going off behind my eyes, I pick up my bag and climb through the bleached-out dunes, each step sinking into the hot sand. Like walking through treacle, Mum said.

I walk down the hill into Churchtown. Hardly a town. A village. A launderette, a pub, and the post office. Our post office. It's still quiet, despite the heat. No real tourists yet, just weekenders and hard-core surfers, sleeping in their vans near the Point, watching and waiting for the perfect wave. People complain, but I like them. Bringing another world into our little one, bigger and brasher and better than our endless wet, gray granite and old Land Rovers. Nothing ever happens here. "Take me with you," I want to say. But I don't. And then I think that Stella is a sort of perpetual tourist, carrying cigarettes and sunglasses and possibility. And I feel that thing inside me again. In my blood. Warm, like the fuzz of alcohol. Stella.

I open the door to the post office, setting off the cowbells. Mrs. Hickman is at the register and Alfie is on the floor, still in his crocodile outfit, reading *Horse & Hound.* He is not especially interested in horses. Or hounds. He just likes magazines. It's the glossy pages and new smell. And facts. He reads pretty much every magazine in the shop every month. *Elle. Caravanning Monthly.* Anything he can reach. Dad puts the *GQ*s on the top shelf now, next to the ones in the plastic bags that only Mental Nigel and some of the farm men get.

Alfie looks up. "Jude, did you know that horses can die from a tummy ache?"

"Wow," I say, not meaning it. "Where's Dad?"

"At the wholesaler's," Mrs. Hickman answers. "Been gone hours. Prob'ly jammed on the A30 again. So how'd it go, luvvie? The exam?"

"Huh . . . ? Oh, fine," I say. But I'm not thinking about exams. Not anymore. I turn back to Alfie. "Did you go to school like that again?" I ask.

Alfie nods.

"Don't look at me," says Mrs. Hickman.

I wasn't, but she carries on anyway. "I said he's got to wear his uniform but he won't flamin' change for me and your dad's already out by then."

"Doesn't matter," I say. "I think it shows character."

Something Mum used to say.

Mrs. Hickman grunts, in obvious disagreement.

I take a bottle of water from the fridge and open it. A perk of living above a shop. Pretty much the only one.

"There's a tap out back," Mrs. Hickman says. "All the water you want. Free."

I ignore her and take a swig.

"You OK, love?" Mrs. Hickman is staring at me. Like I've done something terrible.

"Fine," I say.

But she's still staring.

"I said I'm fine."

"OK. OK. Just making sure." She waves her hand as if to dismiss me and goes back to filling the chewing gum stand.

I want to tell someone. Anyone. The secret is bursting in me. Begging to be let out. I look at Alfie on the floor. And crouch down next to him.

"Stella's back," I say.

"Who?" Alfie raises his eyes from the magazine.

"The girl who came in earlier. Tall. Blonde. Long hair?" Alfie looks blank. "Kind of like Kate Moss. But not as skinny. She said you told her I was at the beach?"

Alfie shrugs and goes back to *Horse & Hound*. He's too young to remember her. One year old when Mum died and Stella came. Two or three when she left.

Dad will remember her, though. And so will Ed. My stomach turns. Nervous. Or excited, maybe.

"Ain't you got a GCSE to study for, missy?" Mrs. Hickman crushes an empty box and pushes it into the bin.

I have. Drama. The last exam. It's a practical— Shakespeare—and it's not for a week. But I take my bag and the water upstairs anyway, glad of the excuse to get away.

Salt of the earth, Dad calls her. "Looked after you and Alfie like you were hers." And she did, I guess. Though she had three of her own too. Brought them with her when she worked in the house. Smelling mumsy in a way Mum never did. Of soap and dough. Wearing a housecoat, sleeves rolled up over pudgy arms, doing the jobs Mum didn't know how to do. Or didn't want to, more like, Mrs. Hickman would say, thinking I was too young to hear. And I'd played with the boys. The youngest, Ed, just two years older than me. He'd grown up on the farm like it was his playground too. He was my best friend. My only friend. Until Stella came.

I flop down on my bed and turn on the CD player. Drums and guitars burst into life and I shut my eyes. Stella is back. Golden Stella. Bright and shining. Lighting me up in her trail. And I am glad. And scared. Because now something might happen.

5

I'M STILL lying there when Stella walks in, four CDs later. Doesn't knock, just flops down on the bed beside me. Wearing this yellow ball gown and smelling of lighter fluid and Doublemint gum.

I sit up, fear and excitement running through me. "God, Stella. You gave me a fright."

Stella shrugs. "Door was open."

"Did Dad see you?"

"Nope. All quiet on the western front." She picks up a CD case and examines it. Throws it back on the stack, dismissing it. "How radical."

I feel my face redden. How does Stella always see through that stuff? Even at the age of ten, she was defacing pop posters and modeling herself on dead actresses. Forties Hollywood starlets, radiating beauty and discontent. She's right about the CD. I bought it because I heard Ed and his mates talking about the band, hoping that by some osmotic process I would be instantly interesting just by owning it.

"Still, better than the stuff your dad listens to, I suppose. All that cheap TV drama ballad stuff gets on my nerves." She picks up my copy of *The Catcher in the Rye* and flicks through it idly. Not really reading. I wait for the comment. But it doesn't come. I feel grateful for, excited by, the silent approval. If that's what it is.

"So, where have you been all this time?" I say.

"Here and there. Bournemouth was the worst. It's shit. Don't ever go." Stella drops the book back on the pile. "Full of old people and yappy little dogs that crap everywhere. Vile."

She turns over onto her stomach. Legs crossed in the air. "Oh. And London. For a year," she adds, as if it is nothing.

"You lived in London? Oh, my God. How come?"

London—the London I remember from Mum's trips, or rare visits to Gran's Belgravia flat, or have imagined from soap operas and pop videos and film sets—is Neverland and Disney World and Dante's *Inferno* rolled into one. A Paradise Found of clothes and clubs and forbidden pleasures.

She ignores me. "It was totally amazing. We were living on the top floor of this five-story building with these

29

musicians underneath and a high-class hooker in the basement. Well, that's what Dad says she was. Seriously. Anyway, Piers—he's one of the musicians—took me to all these gigs. . . . You won't believe who I snogged after one of them."

"Who?"

"Johnny Gillespie"

I don't know who he is. But I know he must be somebody. Somebody bright and brilliant. "Liar," I say.

"Did too. Outside the Rocket. He was horrible. Breath was totally rank."

"So why'd you do it, then?"

"Because I could, duh." Stella rolls onto her side. "So, what about you?"

"What about me?"

"Who have you snogged?"

I feel the butterflies in my stomach unfurl their wings. Stella has been everywhere, seen everything. I have been nowhere. Seen nothing but the narrow streets of Churchtown and the bleak rocks of the Point.

"Um. No one, really." I dig around desperately in my head. Trying to unearth something to show her. To prove I'm not who she thinks I am. Who everyone thinks I am. "Well, Woody. You know, Julian Wood, from school? Once. At the fair. But—" It's not good enough.

"Christ, don't tell me you're still a virgin." Stella looks at me in amazement. Or worse, delight. "You are, aren't you? I knew it."

I could lie. Tell her I'm not. Pick some random name. A boy from town. Tell her I've done it. That it was nothing. That he meant nothing. But that's not me. And she knows it. "So?"

"Nothing. Just . . . I mean, are you, like, all 'What Would Jesus Do?' or something?"

"No. I'm just . . . picky. You know. High standards." I try to joke. "Have you seen most of the boys around here?" It is true. Kind of. I would rather die than let any of the farm boys or yachties near me. They're repellent in equal measure. But none of them try anyway. Why would they?

"OK. Million-dollar question."

I groan. This is Stella's favorite game. Absurd, unanswerable questions. A choice of two evils.

"Who'd you rather—"

"Hang on." I can hear someone on the stairs. Alfie? No, too heavy. I spring up and pull the lock across.

"Jude?"

Dad. I don't want him to know about Stella. Not yet. Maybe not ever. Because he hated her then. Hated all the things I loved. The way she looked, the way she spoke. The way she was. Different. Daring. And she hasn't changed now.

I take a breath. "Mmm?"

"Ed's here," he says.

"Ed? What, Fat Ed?" hisses Stella.

"Shh," I hiss.

"Jude, have you got someone in there?"

"Yeah. I mean, no. Um, hang on. I'll be down in a second."

Stella is wide-eyed, grinning. "Let me come!"

"No way," I mouth.

"Pretty please!" she begs.

"No." I shake my head.

"Jude?" Dad is still there.

"Coming," I shout. Then, quieter, for Stella's benefit, because it's what she would say, "Jesus." I stretch the word out. Watch it hang in the air. I feel that heat again. Electricity. And I know what a drug must feel like. Because I know then that this is the beginning of a bittersweet addiction.

I hear the stairs again. "Just wait here," I say to Stella. "Read a book or something." She smiles. And I know she won't. That this is theater for her. This is what she lives for. "Just be quiet, anyway."

"As a mouse." She crosses her heart. Hopes to die. And I believe her. I trust her.

But Ed won't. He never did. And I know I am about to lie again.

Ed is sitting on the wall by the back door, feet on his skateboard, wheeling it from side to side. I sit next to him.

"Hey, Jude," he sings.

I wince. Knowing that she is watching. Listening. "God, Ed. Don't you ever get bored of that?"

Ed grins. "Nope. So how'd the French go?"

"*Magnifique*," I say.

"Seriously?"

"No. It was fine, you know. I'll pass. Not A-plus pass, I mean. Just pass." And they're my words. The words Jude would pick. But the tone is different. It's not "I'll be OK. Don't worry about me." It's "What's it to you, anyway?" The way Stella would say it.

Ed pauses for a second, two wheels of his skateboard in the air. "Are you OK?"

It's happening already. I can feel it. But I can't tell him. I won't. I don't need the lecture. Not from Dad and certainly not from him.

"I'm fine," I say.

"Sure. Exams. I know." He lets the wheels slap on the ground. "Listen. Do you want to come down the Point later? There's a load of us going."

I'm surprised. Not because we never go there. We do. Summer after summer we've spent there watching the tourists down below on the beach. But this is different. Because his friends will be there. And my enemies. The Plastics.

"Um, maybe. I don't know. You know Dad."

"Well, if you want to, we'll be there at eight."

"OK. Thanks," I say.

"Listen, I've got to go." Ed flips the board effortlessly and catches it with one hand as he stands. He drops his head to one side, dark hair hanging over his eye. "Try to come later, yeah?"

"I will."

But I know I won't. I never do. Not when the others are there. I have a million excuses. Dad. Exams. Emily Applegate. And one more now.

Stella.

When I get back upstairs, Stella is lying on the bed, smoking.

"Stella! Not in here. He'll smell it. At least open the window."

"God, chill." She stubs the cigarette out on a CD cover. "So, when did he stop being fat, anyway?"

I look at her.

"Saw him out the window. He's a Baldwin."

"Pardon?"

"He's hot." She smiles.

"What? Ed?" I look out at his retreating figure, T-shirt, board shorts, and Vans, walking up the hill, skateboard in one hand. Ed, who I dropped like a hot coal when Stella arrived the first time, because she said he couldn't be in our gang because he was too fat, an embarrassment. Ed, who hung around anyway, quietly waiting until Stella was gone. Who let me stay at his house when I tried to run away. Who taught me to surf. Who walked me to the gate on my first day at Duchy. And was waiting for me there when the bell rang at the end of the day. Who patiently told me I was perfect every time Emily Applegate called me a freak, or a bitch, or a mental case.

"I don't know." And I don't. I can't remember when his hair got long, or he stopped wearing lace-ups and bought old-skool trainers. Or when he got the board. Then I realize. My stomach lurches. "No, Stella. He's out of bounds. Totally. I mean it."

"Jeez. OK." She makes a face. "Anyone would think you fancied him."

"No . . ." And I mean it. It's not that. It's Stella. And what she might do. "It's just . . . you know. He's my mate. And, anyway, he's leaving in a few months. Going to study law at King's College."

"Great, another corporate fat cat in a pinstripe. Just what the world needs."

"No. Ed's not like that. . . . He's going to do good stuff." And he is. Going to change the world, he says. From the inside.

"Whatever. So, million-dollar question. Who'd you rather? Fat Ed or that bloke who sits outside the launderette all day?"

"What, Mental Nigel?"

"Whatever. Is that his name?"

"Yeah . . . Well, not the mental bit. No, not him. He's totally weird. Ugh."

"So, Fat Ed, then."

"No . . . oh, I guess. Christ, Stella. This game is stupid."

"No, it's not. You want to do Fat Ed. Deal with it. Come on, my turn."

I don't argue with her. Not because she's right. But because she will win. "OK. Mental Nigel or Mr. Applegate?"

"Easy. Mr. Applegate."

"Gross. Why?"

"He's rich. I could blackmail him not to tell Emily. Or his wife."

"You are sick."

Stella smiles. "I hope so."

Alfie shouts up the stairs. "Dad says tea in five minutes."

"'Kay . . ." I turn to Stella. "Sorry."

She shrugs. "Got to fly, anyway. Want to go shopping tomorrow?"

I shake my head. "School. I've got this drama rehearsal thing. The exam's next week."

"You'll totally pass. You were always into that acting stuff."

And then I tell her. Because then there will be no going back. Because she will make it happen. "I'm applying to the Lab. You know, in London? For September. I mean, I haven't sent the letter yet. And then I might not even get an audition. But—"

"You're leaving? What does Tom have to say about that?"

She means Dad.

"He doesn't know. Not yet." He'll lose it. Thinks I'm too young. Thinks I'm trying to be like her. "But I'm sixteen," I say, convincing myself more than Stella. "And it's not like I'll be living in some crack den. I can stay at Gran's." I can do this. "Anyway, I have to get out of this place, or I'll end

36

up stuck here like Mrs. Hickman, stacking shelves till I'm sixty."

And it sounds good, like that. Like I mean it. Not like I'm terrified. Not like I know that there are only three places left this year, only open to special cases. The ones who live abroad. Or were ill. Or were so scared they missed the audition in March. Not like this is Last-Chance Saloon.

"So why haven't you posted it?" Stella says. "The application."

"I don't know." And right then I don't. Don't know why I doubted myself. Because this is what Stella does. Makes me strong.

"Give it here." She sits up.

"What?"

"The application form. Give it to me. I'm going to send it."

And I do. I dig deep into my drawer, under the bits of paper that record who I am, who I was, the school reports and drawings and cards, until I feel it, the letter, crackling with promise. She takes it. Puts it down the front of her dress.

"Safest place," she says.

Then someone shouts up the stairs again. "Jude. How many times? Dinner!" Not Alfie this time. Dad.

"OK!" I shout. And, under my breath, "For God's sake."

"Time for tea, children," says Stella as she unwraps another stick of gum.

We walk down the stairs to the door. I look at her, chewing, sunglasses on, scuffed toes kicking an invisible stone, and wish I looked like that. Bored. Above it.

"See you after school?" I say.

"Not if I see you first." She smiles and walks off. The letter down inside her ball gown. My possibility against her heart.

"Ha, ha," I drawl. But part of me is scared she means it. And I don't want her to go. Not when I've just gotten her back.

6

SHE COMES the next day. I'm at school, sitting under the oak tree on the field. Eating cold chicken, left over from last night. As far away from Emily Applegate and the Plastics — from noncivilization — as possible. From the toilets where they've flushed my head in the cracked and stained bowl; from the lockers where they've slammed my fingers in the door; from the cafeteria, where they've tripped me and spilled Coke on my uniform. But they still find me. I watch them walking toward me, like some slo-mo Gap commercial. All blond ponytails, tanned legs, and bleached white teeth. I feel my stomach turn and a wave of dizziness wash over me. They stop, photo-shoot perfect, in front of me.

Emily speaks first. That's how it works. "Nice lunch."

"That's gross." Dawce looks in disgust as a piece of chicken falls out of my mouth, the grease staining my white shirt.

I wipe it away quickly. "Shut up."

Emily smiles. "Wow. Clever put-down. How long did it take you to think that one up?"

The Plastics snigger.

"Why do you care what I eat, anyway?" I say.

"Oh, I don't. Just confirms your fruitcake status, though."

"Whatever." Out loud I'm above it. But inside I'm begging them, *Just leave me alone. Please.*

"Again, genius."

"Just go away, will you?" I plead.

"Or what?"

Or nothing. That's the problem. I can't run to Mummy. And for all the blah in the school rulebook about bullying, the teachers don't do anything. "If you give off signals that you don't want to belong, people will make sure you don't." Beautiful. All you can do is keep your head down and hope they'll find some Year Seven with a lisp to pick on instead.

But then there's a noise behind me. The smell of lighter fluid and Doublemint. And Stella is there. Out of nowhere. My fairy godmother. Wearing an Alice-in-Wonderland headband in her backcombed hair and some vintage dress, all pink puffball skirt and tight top.

"What's your damage, Applegate?"

Emily stares. "My damage? How retro."

"Seriously, Emily . . . Emily—" Stella stops like she's pondering the word. "That's a fat girl's name, really."

"I'm not fat."

"Not yet," Stella concedes. "Give it five years, though. You'll be shopping in menswear like your mum."

"Bitch," Emily snaps, searching for a comeback. She finds one. "At least my mum's alive. Not some dead mental case."

But Stella can do better. "Truly Shakespearian. Now who's shit at put-downs?"

Emily snorts. "Whatever."

Holly Harker tugs at her arm. "Come on, Em."

Emily snatches her arm back. "Get off me."

Holly drops her hand. Emily stares at me and then laughs. Short and catty. Then she walks away. Half the school watching her stride across the field. The Plastics flanking her like My Little Bodyguards.

"Advantage, me."

Stella. I turn to her. "What was that all about?"

Stella pops her gum. "Gee, thanks, Stella. Oh, that's OK, Jude. Anytime."

"Sorry. I didn't mean . . ." I feel a stab of fear again. That I've upset her. That she'll turn on me like they did. "It's just that . . . they don't like me already."

"They don't even like each other. Oh, hang on. What? So you want them to like you? Christ. Why do you want

41

to hang out with a load of Psycho Barbies and Diet Coke–heads, anyway?"

"I don't. I just don't want it to get worse." I look down. Waiting for her to trash me. To write me off as a loser. A weakling. But she doesn't. Instead she smiles and holds out her dress like the angel on top of the Christmas tree.

"It's all right. I'm here now. I'm your knight in shining armor. Your fairy bloody godmother."

"Ha, ha."

"Seriously. With me around, she'll back off eventually." Stella takes the gum out and sticks it to the tree.

"Maybe." But I don't believe it. "What are you doing here, anyway? If the teachers see you —"

"What? They'll ask me nicely to leave? Give you detention? Big deal." She pulls a packet of cigarettes out of her bag.

"Stella!"

"We're outside. Jesus. Chill, would you?" She lights one up. "So, what are we going to do about Emily?"

"I don't know." I shrug. "Nothing?"

"Wrong answer," retorts Stella. "Come on, Jude. She needs to learn a lesson. Like the ponytail. But bigger. And better. And badder."

"No, Stella. Leave it. It's not worth it," I plead.

"Bollocks. She's a plastic bitch and she's going to pay for it. I just need to figure out how."

"But —"

"No buts. Here, hold this." She hands me her cigarette.

"My bra strap's all twisted."

Then I get that feeling. You know. Like you are being watched.

"Jude?"

I look up, panicked. Oh, God. My drama teacher, Mr. Hughes. I glance at Stella with what I hope is a "Just don't say anything, don't even look at him, and cover up your bra" look. Stella ignores me and smiles at him. A Cheshire-cat-that-got-the-cream smile. Mr. Hughes says nothing. But he's seen it. Seen her.

"So, Jude." But he's looking at Stella still, distracted. Seconds pass. Then it's as if he returns from another place. Back to me. "You were great this morning."

"Oh . . . right. Thanks." I wonder if he's just saying that or if he really means it. If I really am good. Good enough to pass the exam. Good enough for the Lab.

"Seriously." He smiles. "You've got no worries."

I nod. Believing him now.

"So, can I expect you in A-level theater later?"

"Sorry?"

"Introduction? This afternoon? I mean, I know you're not coming back." He laughs. "But in case you change your mind. Decide to slum it with us for another two years . . ."

"Right. Yeah, I think so."

"Great. Great." He pauses. "You'll want to give that up, though. Bad for the voice. Unless you want to sound like Bob Dylan. Which I'm guessing you don't."

I look at the cigarette, still burning between my fingers.

"Oh, God. Sorry . . . I mean, sorry for saying God as well."
I glare at Stella but she's looking at Mr. Hughes. "It's not
mine. Really. I . . ."

He smiles. "Well. OK. Good." He turns to go, then
stops and glances over his shoulder at us. "Oh. And don't
let anyone else catch you looking like that. I know it's only
a few weeks, but uniform is uniform."

I nod, gormlessly, as he heads back toward the quad.
Then stare down at my shirt, my kilt. Regulation. He must
mean Stella. Must think she's a Duchy girl. As if. I turn to
her. "Thanks a bloody million. You could have told him it
was yours."

But Stella isn't listening. "Oh, my God. He is gorgeous."
"Stella!"

"What? He is." She looks at me, smiles. "Oh, don't tell
me you don't fancy him. You're so bloody transparent."

And I am. It's like she can see inside me. See every
dirty secret that lurks in the darkness. But that was finished long ago. It never even started. It was just a crush.
Childish. Pathetic. And I knew he wouldn't. And nor
would I.

"No way. He's got a girlfriend. Anyway, he's old."

"What is he? Thirty? That's not old."

"Stella!"

"He is, though, isn't he?" Stella elbows me, grinning.
"A babe, I mean."

I pause.

"Kind of . . ." I admit.

Because he is. Hair curling over the neckband of his washed-out concert T-shirt. Old tweed jacket and jeans. Skin turning brown from the June sun. Not like the other teachers in their navy-blue suits and Ford Mondeos.

I watch him disappear into the theater building, the doors swinging shut behind him. Then I turn to her. "You'd better go, Stell. He's right. If anyone else sees you, I'll be in detention for a week."

She stubs her cigarette out on the scorched grass. "School's out for summer."

"Not at Duchy it's not." Never mind that we're on exam leave. Or that half of us won't even be back in the autumn. Duchy girls breathe rules. And Stella has broken at least three.

She's silent for a second. Then I see it. A flicker in her eyes. A dare. "Come with me," she urges.

"Where?" I don't get it.

"I don't know. Anywhere. Just out of here." She pauses. "The dunes."

"Now?"

"Yeah." She's standing now, right hip stuck out, looking up from under her lashes. "What have you got this afternoon?"

"Um. Supposed to have this A-level introduction thing."

"What's the point of that? You're not even staying."

"Well . . ." She's right. And even if I did stay, it's not like I don't know exactly how it's going to be. Same corridors. Same teachers. Same Emily Applegate. Just without the uniform.

Stella is already walking backward to the gate, beckoning me to follow. "Come on."

And I realize I want to go. Old Jude wouldn't. She would stay at school. Sit quietly through the blah talk. But that's not who I want to be. So I follow her. Because I can. Because she makes me feel like someone else. Someone who can walk out of school when she likes. Someone who can be just like her.

7

WE STAYED in the dunes until four. Timed it so Dad would think I'd just gotten off the bus, back from school. Hoped he wouldn't notice the sand in my hair, on my kilt, trailing from my shoes. She sits on the wall outside, sucking a Popsicle, watching me go in.

Then she's gone. For a week. A week where I rehearse my lines. Practice for hours in front of the mirror. Being someone else. Isabella, from *Measure for Measure*. A nun. *How appropriate,* I think.

And I should be grateful that she stays away, lets me work. But I'm not. Because I miss her. She's been gone nearly eight years and back just days and already I don't know how I managed without her. I need her.

So I made her promise to come back.

And she does.

She's waiting for me after my exam. Outside the dressing room. I'm wiping makeup off my face when I smell it. Lighter fluid and gum. And my heart jumps. The lurch of seeing a new love. Or a lost one. At least, that's what I read once. I pull on my uniform and run out into the corridor, scared I'll miss her. That someone else will see her first and she'll have to go.

But she's still there, leaning against the wall in this fifties sundress with cherries on it.

She sticks her gum to the peeling paint of the door frame and smiles. "Ready?"

"For what?"

But it doesn't matter. I don't care what it is. Today I'll do it.

"You've got to stop dressing like a bloody schoolgirl," Stella says as she pulls my kilt down for me. We're in the changing room at Dixie's, this vintage shop on Ship Street in town. A shop I've walked past a dozen times. Wishing I were the kind of person who would wear clothes like that. Clothes that shout, "I'm different! I'm somebody!"

I laugh, letting her undress me. "This is my uniform," I protest.

"I don't mean that," she says.

And I know what she's talking about. Even out of

school, I dress to disappear. Shapeless jumpers. Jeans. Faded T-shirts. Until now.

She smiles, pulls the black silk down over my head. Zips it up. Dressing me like a doll. Then her smile drops. "Oh, God, Jude."

"What?" I'm worried now. Worried that I was wrong. That I can't pull it off.

But she's shaking her head. "Look."

She spins me around to see what she's done. To see her staggering genius. I look. I'm in this sixties A-line number, hair pulled back, feet pushed into patent heels.

"Why, Miss Polmear," Stella breathes, "you really are beautiful." And I laugh. And Stella puts her arms around me. And we look at the reflection in the mirror. At this new person standing there. She is strange and strong and beautiful. And she is me.

The dress costs thirty pounds. Stella lends me the money.

"You can owe me," she says.

I'm not sure I want to owe Stella anything. But I want the dress. Have to have it. "I'll pay you back," I say. And I will. I still have birthday money from Gran left over in my account.

I go to unzip it. But Stella has other ideas. "Keep it on," she says. "You'll need it."

"Where are we going?"

"Out."

* * *

"You'll be fine," Stella says. "You look old. At least twenty." But my heart still pounds when we walk into the pub.

"Just look bored," she instructs. "And hold these. Put them on the bar." She hands me her Marlboro Reds.

I do as I'm told. I fumble, though, dropping the packet on the floor. Cigarettes roll across the tiles. But the barman doesn't miss a beat when I ask for a vodka and tonic. A thrill surges through me. I'm drunk before it even touches my lips.

"Over there," Stella says, nodding to the corner.

We sit down in a booth, away from the stares and leers of the men with their pints and *Racing Times*.

"Hardly Soho, is it?" she says. "But it'll do."

"Yeah," I say. Like I'd know. I take a gulp of vodka. It stings my throat, but then quinine sweetness takes over.

Stella picks up her cigarettes. Pulls one out and lights it. "So, million-dollar question." She pauses, punctuating her sentence with a purposeful drag. "Would you rather be deaf or blind?"

"Um. I don't know." And I'm thinking, *What would Stella say?* I pick one. "Deaf?"

Bingo.

"Me too." She exhales, the smoke curling toward me. I breathe it in, wondering if it will make me feel different. High.

She cocks her head. "Want to know why?"

I nod.

"I could still see to do my makeup. Deaf people always

dress better than blind ones." I start. Something I once thought, then hated myself for. And she knows it. She meets my eyes. A look of recognition. Of power.

Then it's gone. She smiles. "And I'd never have to listen to bloody Radio 2 again. Jesus, what is with Tom and that station?"

I smile. "I know. Awful, isn't it?"

She laughs. "Your turn."

I take another mouthful of vodka. Let the heat run down my throat and into my stomach, into my blood. "OK," I say, playing her at her own game. "Midget or giant?"

Four hours later, I stagger down the steps of the bus, my legs heavy, my uniform in a ball in my bag. Ed is there, in the shelter, waiting to go God knows where. Where is there to go around here, anyway?

For a second he doesn't recognize me. I am a stranger. Then he sees who it is inside the disguise. "Jude? Where'd you get that?" He is looking at my dress, cut low over my breasts.

Self-consciousness seeps back into my veins, cold and sobering. "Why? Don't you like it?"

"No . . . I do. It's just . . . different."

I am relieved. Grasping at approval. Though Stella wouldn't give a damn what anyone else thought.

"Where've you been?" he asks.

"Cornish Arms. End of exams thing." Like it's nothing. But Ed knows better. "Who with?"

"With whom," I retort. Then quieter, "No one you'd know," I lie.

"Have you been drinking?"

"Yeah. So? You drink." He does. They all do. Up on the Point. Beer and cider and stuff. But not vodka. Not Ed.

"I'm eighteen."

"What, and I'm a baby?"

"No. It's just that I'm not used to you . . . like this." He is silent for a while. I can hear the blood rushing to my head. I feel dizzy.

"You look good, though," he concludes.

I feel my stomach turning. "Got to go." I stumble out of the bus shelter and up the street, drawing in deep lungfuls of air to stop the vomit rising. Can't be sick with air in your lungs. One of Alfie's facts. I make it back to the post office, thanking God it's early closing. Dad and Alfie are in the kitchen, door shut. I run up the stairs to the bathroom and stick my head under the tap, the cold water running down my cheeks in rivulets. I gulp it down. Got to sober up.

An hour later, I'm sitting at the table, pushing frozen fish pie and tinned sweet corn around my plate. Dad is watching me. Wondering if I've got an eating disorder, probably. Another anorexic casualty from Duchy.

"Guess what?" says Alfie.

"What?" I sigh.

"The till was short today. Mrs. Hickman might have stolen—"

"Alfie!" Dad snaps.

"What? She might have."

"Mrs. Hickman didn't steal anything. It's a mistake. That's all." I can feel Dad's eyes on my dress. I think of Stella. Then immediately feel guilty. Stella hasn't even been in the shop. And she wouldn't. And Mrs. Hickman is always getting change wrong.

"So, Jude. Going to tell me what you're wearing?"

"A dress," I say out loud. And in my head, *Duh.*

"New, though. Where'd you get the money?"

I look at him. Trying to see inside, like she can with me. "Are you accusing me of stealing?"

"No. I just asked. It's not like you to buy stuff like that, is it?"

"I've got money. From Gran." I stab a sweet-corn kernel with my fork.

But he won't give up. "So, who'd you go with? Shopping, I mean."

And for one minute I want to tell him. Because I know he wants me to have a friend. But not one like her. And I remember last time. Dad shouting. Telling her to go away.

"No one," I say. "Just me."

I fork a prawn and put it into my mouth. Willing it to stay down. Waiting for him to challenge me. But the phone rings and I'm saved. Maybe my fairy godmother does exist after all.

"We'll talk about this later." He goes into the hallway, taking his glass with him.

"Whatever," I say, and push my plate away.

"Dad, Jude whatevered you!"

"Shut up, Alfie." I kick at his legs.

But he's too fast. My foot arcs into nothing.

He is staring at me still. Fascinated. Thinking.

"Were you with Stella?" he asks.

I look at him blankly. How does he know? Then I remember. I told him she was back, that day in the dunes. I nod.

His face lights up with the lie I have told. "But you said you were on your own."

"You wouldn't understand." I push a kernel across the table and watch it roll silently onto the floor. "He wouldn't understand. He doesn't like her. She did some stuff."

"What stuff?"

"Just stuff . . ." So much stuff. And I shouldn't tell him. But I want someone to know who she is. How incredible she is. Why I want her, need her. "Like . . . she painted the toilet red."

"Really?"

I nod. She did. And the bath. One Sunday when Dad was in the top field with a calving. Stella was delighted. Said it was like peeing into blood. But Dad went spare. Made me scrape it all off.

"What else, what else?"

But I don't answer. I'm listening to Dad on the phone, talking about shop awnings. God, the glamour of it. And I think about London and Stella kissing that guy outside the Rocket. And I remember Mum telling me she once kissed some pop star at the Palais. Because she could. And I want to get out of this town, out of this life, like never before. The need is overwhelming.

8

THE LETTER arrives on Saturday. Exams over, the long summer stretches out before me. I'm behind the till, making minimum wage, Stella sitting beside me, flicking through *Vogue* and passing judgment on society.

The cowbells tinkle. Stella looks up.

"Oh, my God. What does she think she's wearing!" she whispers.

It's Mrs. Penleaze. Forty-something. No makeup. Hair scraped back in a lank ponytail. Anorak, despite the heat, and flowery skirt.

"She looks like a bag lady."

I let out a snigger and Mrs. Penleaze looks at me, frowning. I turn it into a cough and smile at her, elbowing Stella to shut her up. Mrs. Penleaze goes back to her agonizing decision between baked beans and Spaghetti Hoops.

"Go on. Take a risk. Get the hoops," whispers Stella again.

"God, Stella. Pack it in."

"Well. Anyone would think she was on *Deal or No Deal* the way she's dragging it out. It's not like it's a life-changing decision."

"Maybe it is for her," I say. "Maybe she's never had spaghetti before."

Stella flashes me a lipstick smile. And I know what she is going to say. "OK. Dare."

"No way." I shake my head.

"Yes way. I dare you to say something about that skirt."

I sigh. "Good or bad?"

"Whatever. Just say something."

Mrs. Penleaze comes to the counter with the beans and a *Western Daily*. Total, £1.10. I don't need to look at the price tags. Know what everything costs. The thought saddens and sickens me.

She hands over some coins. Stella elbows me.

I can't say anything bad. Just can't. But I have to say something. What comes out is, "That's a lovely skirt." It's pathetic, and I know it. And so does Stella. But I have done the dare, and that's what matters.

Mrs. Penleaze looks down, confused.

"Oh . . . um . . . thank you, Jude."

"It's a . . . er . . . bold choice. Suits you." I drop ten

pence into her hand and slam the till drawer shut.

"So. Tell your dad hello." She tries out a smile.

"I will. Call again soon." I am choking down the laughter.

"Have a nice day," adds Stella. Perfect all-American service with a smile.

The door closes and Stella and I shriek.

"You've probably made her day," says Stella. "I bet she hasn't had a compliment for years. Poor cow. Not that she deserves one in that getup."

"Not as bad as Mr. Penleaze, though. Have you seen his ears?"

"God. Imagine them in bed," ponders Stella.

"That's gross, Stella. I don't want to."

"Oh, Janet," she pants. "I love you, Janet. Do it to me, Janet!"

"Shut up!"

"You're right. They probably don't bother. Just pick each other's corns or something."

"Stop it now." I hit her with a copy of *Cosmopolitan,* but she still has *Vogue.* Twice as heavy.

The cowbells go again. We stop and look up. I'm praying it's not Mrs. Applegate, all Barbour jacket and Hunters, fighting a losing battle against the scales. Or Mental Nigel, who comes in for sweets and magazines. *Playboy* and penny chews. Stella would have a field day. But it's neither. It's the postman. How stupid is that? That the post gets delivered here. To a post office. They should drop it off when they open up the mailbox in the morning or something. Different jobs, Jude, Dad says. But it still seems dumb to me.

"All right, Jude?" The postman nods. "One for you here." He hands over a stack of envelopes. Bills. Except for one. Thick, white vellum, A4 size, logo printed on the top left-hand corner. The Lab. My legs feel weak. And I'm not sure if it's because I'm scared that I haven't gotten an audition or scared that I have.

"I hope it's good news. Anyway, best be off. No rest for the wicked, eh?" He laughs, a throaty, guttural sound. "See you later, love."

But I am still staring at the envelope.

"Earth to Jude . . ." he says.

"What?" I look up. He's smiling at me, waiting. "Oh, right. Yeah . . . See you . . . Thanks."

"Another world," he mutters as he leaves.

The envelope feels hot in my hand. Dangerous. Life-changing. The opposite of Mrs. Penleaze's beans.

"Jesus! Would you just open it, Jude?"

But I can't. Not in front of Stella. I don't want her to see if I don't get in. Don't want to be a nobody in front of her.

"Well, if you won't . . ." Stella snatches the envelope from me.

"Give it back. It's private."

She tuts. "What do you mean, private? I tell you everything."

"Stella! Come on, give it back."

She's holding it above her head. "You didn't say, 'Simon says.'"

"What?"

Stella raises an eyebrow.

"Oh, for . . . Simon says, 'Give it back.'"

"Only if you open it now."

"OK . . . God!"

Stella holds it out. I snatch it. Still hot. My fingers are shaking as I run them under the flap and pull out the two stapled sheets.

"What?" Stella demands.

"Wait." I scan down the page for the bad news. And again to make sure. But it isn't there. They want to see me.

I look up. "I've got an audition."

"Let me see!"

I hand it over.

"Oh, my God. Look at the date." She is wide-eyed and helpless with happiness. "It's in two weeks."

"I know." I make a face.

Stella grins. And I laugh, infected with her delight.

She claps her hands to her chest. *"O Romeo, Romeo! wherefore art thou Romeo?"*

"Shut up!" I smile. "I'm not doing that, anyway. Too clichéd. And I'm hardly Juliet."

"Yeah, you are. All innocent . . ." She lingers on the word, savoring it.

"I'm doing Isabella again. Same as the GCSE."

"A nun! Even better. I bet Mr. Hughes loves that. Imagining you in your penguin outfit. Or out of it . . ."

"God, Stella. Is that all you think about?"

"Yup. Mostly. That and vodka. Decadence is so this year. Says so in the Bible." She waves *Vogue* at me. "So, this calls for a party."

"Yeah. I guess."

"I guess? It's Saturday night. You're going to drama school."

"Might be."

"Bugger *might be*. You're going."

Then it hits me. And it's like in films when you see the background rushing toward someone. The world is turning around me. I feel the blood drain from my face. This is it. My chance. And I'm terrified and exhilarated. Because it's everything I've wanted for so long. To go somewhere. To be somebody. I want this feeling, this day, to last forever.

"The Point," she says.

"What?"

"Tonight. Let's go there, me and you." Stella has a plan.

"OK . . ." But then I remember something. Heard some kids talking about it in the shop. "No. Wait. We can't. There's this party up there."

"Even better." She smiles.

"No, but—"

"But nothing. There'll be vodka, right?"

I nod. And dope, I think. And Emily Applegate and the Plastics. And all those same million reasons why I shouldn't go. But then I think of Ed. And I want to tell him. To know what he thinks. To see if he's pleased for me, proud of me. And I'm high again on possibility. I want to dance, to drink, to kiss someone. Anyone. Maybe.

"Well . . ." Stella drawls, playing it cool. "I think we should grace them with our presence." Then she shrieks again. And we're hugging, jumping up and down, shouting. Breathless, I feel more alive than I have ever been.

Then Dad bangs on the wall. We fall apart.

"Shit. Tom," says Stella. "You've got to tell him."

"Yeah," I say. "I know."

Stella sighs. "OK. So, gotta go, pussycat." She takes a packet of Marlboro Reds off the shelf behind her. "Take it out of what you owe me, yeah?"

"OK . . . Wait!" I say. "Pick me up? At eight?"

"Half seven," she replies. "Then I can help you get ready."

I feign horror. "Are you saying I can't get dressed by myself?"

"Yup."

"Fair point," I concede. "Half seven, then. Bring makeup."

"OK. Bring booze."

I laugh. "See you."

"Wouldn't want to be you."

And she's gone. I'm alone again. But this time it's different. Everything is different.

The shop is empty, so I slip out the back, letter dazzling white in my hand. Dad's in the stockroom, listening to some twangy folk music about shipwrecks and white hares. *You should be proud of where you come from,* he says. But it's not where you come from, is it? It's where you're going. That's what matters. London. Johnny Gillespie and the Rocket and a high-class hooker in the basement.

I hear a sound above the fiddles and drums. Talking. Dad's on the phone. I listen in. Just in case. Once I got lucky. It was a woman. Rachel, she was called. Worked at the wholesaler's. I met her when she dropped Dad off one day. She wore Mrs. Hickman clothes. Her hair was short. Not even elfin, just short. She smelled of cheap perfume and said she tap-danced. Giggled, like it was exotic, amazing. And I thought of Mum's hobbies. How they changed by the week. Phases, Dad called them. She would take up yoga, then beekeeping, then Buddhism. Trying everything on for size. Trying to find something that would fill the emptiness.

I hated Rachel, and said so. Dad never saw anyone after that. Said we weren't ready. He wasn't ready. So now he just works. And has his nightly drink.

I hear his voice rise above the music. It's nothing. Nobody. And I feel the grip around my throat and chest

63

again. This suffocating house. Town. Life. And I know that I won't tell him. Not now. In case he spoils it. This perfect day.

I pull the door shut, fold the letter, stuff it into the pocket of my jeans, and go back to the Spaghetti Hoops and the papers and the endless clutching monotony of his world.

9

"BLOODY HELL, Jude. Come on!" Stella is leaning on the gate, one hand on her hip, the other tight around the neck of a half liter of vodka. £4.99. Second shelf down, next to the cherry brandy.

I'm struggling up the path in a pair of three-inch Mary Janes and the black dress. Not really outdoor wear. But Stella just says, "Lily Allen wore a wedding dress to Glastonbury." So I don't argue.

Told Dad I was going to see Ed. Just not where. Or who else would be there. Only half a lie, then.

I trip on a clump of grass and twist my ankle. "Ow . . . oh, shit . . . I told you I should have worn boots."

"Take them off, then." Stella unscrews the cap and

swigs back a mouthful. "You can go barefoot. Like the hippies." She twirls around, her tulle skirt sticking out like a ballerina's. Or a fairy. She is Tinkerbell. On crack. Which makes me who? Wendy?

I unstrap the shoes and put them in my bag on top of the cans of lager and the jumper I brought (on the grounds that there is nothing decadent or sexy in dying from hypothermia). The path is dusty underfoot. My ankle hurts, and I know I'll tread on glass or mud or something worse on the way home. But right now, I just want to get there. I reach the gate and we climb over, and onto the Point.

It is wide and long. Covered in grass, its rocky tips stretching out like fingers, stroking the sea. It seems friendly, benign. And during the day it is. Bathed in sunshine, its skin alive with walkers in candy-colored rain ponchos. But that's not where we're going. Beyond the fence that keeps the tourists in are the ledges. Three platforms going down the cliffs. Salt-spattered. Worn flat by the tides. And by surfers and smokers and daredevils, watching the waves, drinking until dawn.

"Ciggy?" Stella holds out the packet she took earlier.

I hesitate for a second. I see him in the stockroom on the phone, among the boxes of cornflakes and tins of soup. Then I see her, Mum, in that photo. Pink heels, cigarette trailing in her hand. And I know which one I want to be. So this time I say yes.

Stella lights it. I take a drag, carefully, trying not to betray my amateur status. It tastes familiar. Of biscuits and bonfires.

It hurts my throat, but I don't cough. I have passed.

"Whose cars are those?" Stella nods down the hill.

I look. A Land Rover, a VW Camper, and a cluster of hatchbacks are parked randomly on the grass.

"Um. The Land Rover's Ed's. Camper van is Matt's. Not sure about the others." Then I see the Mini Cooper. Red convertible. Still shining new. My stomach lurches. Because if he's here, so is she. Then I feel the cigarette between my fingers. The dry grass beneath my bare feet. And I remember who I am. Tonight, at least. *I can do this,* I think. And, anyway, she's the least of my worries. It's Ed I should be afraid of. Of what he'll say when he sees Stella.

"Blair Henderson. The Mini, I mean. It's Blair's."

"Who's Blair Henderson?"

"Yachtie. Goes to County Boys'. Daddy owns a marina." I look at Stella. "He's going out with Emily Applegate, before you start getting any ideas."

"Moi?" Stella mouths. "As if. Anyway, why's he hanging out with Ed? Or, why's Ed hanging out with him?"

"He's not. They both know Matt. He's in Ed's band and Blair gets dope off him. . . . Plus there's no one else to hang out with around here, is there?"

"Well, there's us now. Come on. Let's plow." She links her arm through mine, and, still smoking, we walk down the grassy hill toward the sea.

"You *are* joking." It is not a question. Emily Applegate stares at me and then turns to Matt. "What is *she* doing here?"

67

"Jude?" Ed looks at me, the same shock on his face as on Emily's. Because I've finally shown up after years of maybes? Or because of who I'm with?

They're on the top ledge. Fifteen or so of them. Cans and bottles already open. Crisps and Mars bars and a spliff being passed around. Everyone dressed in jeans. My stomach flutters again. Like I've been told to come to a fancy dress party but the joke is on me. At least I took the shoes off.

Emily sneers. "It's poor little Cinderella. All dressed up for the ball."

Dawce laughs.

I open my mouth to speak, but it's Stella's voice I hear. "God, Emily. You're so predictable."

"At least I'm not mental."

"Oh, give it a rest." Stella lights up another cigarette.

Emily turns to Blair to back her up. But he isn't looking at her anymore. He's staring at Stella. The way men stare when they see someone like her. Stella smiles at him. The corners of his mouth crease. And he's talking to Emily, but his eyes don't move for a second from Stella's face. "Yeah, Emily. Don't be such a bitch."

Everyone is silent for a few seconds, and all we can hear is the sound of the sea and music from someone's iPod speakers. Then Emily snorts. "Give me that." She grabs the spliff off Blair.

He smiles and looks at her finally. "That's what I love about you."

Then he kisses her, taking the smoke into his mouth and breathing it out again. Blow back.

"Jude? Want to sit down?"

I realize I've been staring at Blair and Emily. The way you stare at car crashes or sex on the telly — horrified but fascinated at the same time. I look away and smile at Ed, relieved that he is here. And that he hasn't recognized Stella. Ed, my big brother. Or something like it.

I drop my bag on the ground and sit between him and Matt, who is busy skinning up.

Ed swirls his beer around in the can and looks at me sideways. "So, how come you *are* here, Jude?" he asks.

"Why, shouldn't I be?" I'm embarrassed. Like the little kid who's snuck downstairs to play with the grown-ups.

"No." He shakes his head. "I don't mean that. It's just . . . you never did before."

I shrug. "There's a first time for everything."

"It *is* good to see you." He nudges me with his elbow.

I smile. Nudge him back. It's OK. I can do this. I can fit in here. "Can I have one?" I say, nodding at the can.

He looks surprised again. And I am surprised, not sure where it came from. But he shrugs and pulls a can off a four-pack and hands it to me.

The beer is warm and metallic. I wish I'd brought lemonade for the vodka instead. Or could swallow it neat like Stella. But I take another mouthful of beer anyway. Dutch courage. That's what Mum always said.

"Anyway, I came to see you."

"Really?" Ed half smiles.

"Yeah. I . . . um . . . I've got some news." I wait for Ed to ask the question. But he doesn't, just looks at me, waiting.

"I've got an audition. For drama school. The Lab."

"The Lab?" I can see Ed processing these two little words. "But that's in London, isn't it?"

"Yeah."

"Right. Well done, I guess . . ."

I sink into myself. *Well done, I guess*? Is that it?

Ed sees me shrink. "Sorry. That's not what I . . . I mean, that's brilliant, Jude. I mean . . . you're brilliant. It's just . . . It's a long way. And your dad . . . He won't let you, will he?"

"I'm sixteen, not six. I can do what I want." But somehow I sound like a six-year-old. Stamping her feet and pouting.

"But even so."

"Thanks for raining on my parade."

"Sorry, Jude. I didn't mean to . . . It's great. Seriously. If you get in — I mean, *when* you get in — we can hang out in London. In Covent Garden. Or Camden. It'll be just like Churchtown."

I smile. "But without the rain."

He laughs. "Or the tractors."

"Or the cows."

"Or Emily Applegate."

I look over at her, lying on Blair's lap, hair fanned out,

Smirnoff Ice in her hand. His arm slung over her shoulder. Hand on her tank top. Can see Stella watching them too. Smoking a cigarette with artful detachment. Vodka already a quarter gone.

"Yeah," says Ed. "Or the Plastics . . . or Blair Henderson."

I laugh and lean on Ed, his body warm under the black of his T-shirt. And I feel safe. And strong. Not the fragile way I feel with Stella, the way that needs bravado, defiance. Just a kind of calm. Ed kisses the top of my head. And I don't move. Just lie against him. Peaceful. Then it's gone. The moment is over. Because Matt has finished skinning up and has handed the joint to Ed.

I'm cold all of a sudden. I sit up and hug my legs, goose pimples stippling the skin. I think about getting my jumper out. But I know what Stella will say.

I watch Ed inhale and wonder how far I can go in this charade.

"Going to offer me some?" I say.

But he doesn't. Instead he laughs, coughing out lungfuls of sweet, heavy smoke. "Your dad would kill me."

And then I know he isn't fooled. Not for a second. I'm still just a kid to him. Always will be.

"Whatever," I spit. I pull the beers out of my bag and open one.

"Easy, Jude," he says.

"Who put you in charge?"

He shakes his head. "Forget it."

I drink long and hard to punctuate the silence.

"Just be you," he says finally.

And I want to say, I am. This *is* me, the new, improved Jude.

But he's known me too long. So I tell him the truth. "That's the last person on earth I want to be."

10

I WAKE up on the floor, doing that whole "Where am I?" thing in my head. Then I see the Doors posters, the shelves with the tacky swimming trophies and Harry Potters. And I remember.

Ed is in bed, asleep, one arm trailing on the floor. I am hot. Too hot. I try to stand up, but for some reason I can't move. Then I realize I am straitjacketed into a brown nylon sleeping bag. The same bag I've slept in a hundred times. The same floor. The same room. *Not like waking up in a stranger's bed,* I think. But we're not kids anymore.

I feel inside the bag to check my clothes. I am still dressed. Can't remember going to bed, though. Can't even remember how I got back here. My stomach churns.

I'm going to be sick. I manage to squirm out of the sleeping bag, like I'm emerging from a cocoon. But I'm not a butterfly. I am vile, a crawling insect. I lurch across the room and out of the door, praying that Mrs. Hickman is already gone. The bathroom is at the end of the landing. I make it in time to throw up across the closed toilet seat.

The next three heaves actually go into the toilet. I clean up with someone's washcloth and a bottle of bleach, then rinse the washcloth and put it back on the edge of the bath. Then think better of it and drop it in the bin, covering it with a toilet-paper roll to hide my crime. My legs are shaking. I pick a toothbrush and turn on the taps. Leaning against the sink, waiting for the water to run cold, I look up into the mirror. My face is pale, my eyes ringed by dark circles, hair messy. The confidence that filled me last night is gone. I am ugly. I am nobody. I clean my teeth and creep back to Ed's room.

He's awake. Sitting up against the headboard. A mirror of Jim Morrison on the wall above.

"Why, Miss Polmear, you really are beautiful," he says. But it's not like when Stella said it. And I don't know if he's laughing with me or at me. So I just crawl back into the sleeping bag and close my eyes. Like it will all go away. But it doesn't.

"Don't you want to know what happened last night?"

And I don't. Not really. Because I know it will be bad. But it comes out anyway. "What?"

Ed smiles. And then I know it's with me. "Nothing," he

says. "Well, not nothing. I mean, you got royally drunk and me and Matt put you in the back of the van."

"You drove?"

"Matt. He doesn't drink."

"Just smokes," I say.

"It's different."

I look at Ed. And I need to know. Need to make sure. "Was I awful?"

"No. I mean, you were totally out of it. But you didn't do anything dodgy."

"What, like dance naked or fight with the Hollys or anything?" I try to joke.

Ed laughs. "Nope."

"Thank God." I clutch myself tighter in the sleeping bag.

"You're a happy drunk," I hear him say. "Kind of nice. Until you passed out, anyway."

I smile. Even though my head is pounding. "I feel terrible."

"You look it."

"Thanks a million."

I close my eyes. I try to see it. There are flashes. Like twisting my ankle, still throbbing, even now. Like the sun setting and someone raising a toast to the god of the sea. But no one could remember who that was. Like Matt kissing Holly Harker. Like Blair's hands, moving inside Emily's top. Like Stella dancing, leaning over the ledge . . . I open my eyes. Oh, my God! Stella. Ed has said nothing, but he must have seen her. So either he didn't recognize her or doesn't care. Or . . .

"Jude."

I start. "What?" I wait for it. For him to say it. Say something.

But it's not that. "Is everything OK?" he asks.

I look at him. He's still smiling, but it's forced now. He's got that "I know you've had a tough time, and it must be really hard" kind of look on his face. The kind I hate.

"Why, shouldn't it be?"

"No. Just . . ." He pauses. Trying to find the words. "The drinking and stuff. It's not like you."

And he's right. It's not like the old Jude. But I'm not her anymore. Don't want to be her. "I told you, I'm not a kid."

"No, but—"

"What are you so worried about, anyway?"

He shakes his head, like I'm stupid. "You, of course."

"Well, I don't need you to worry about me. I'm fine."

"Right. That's why you're here at, what?" He looks at his watch. "Eleven on a Sunday morning, hung over and looking like seven kinds of shit."

"Eleven?"

"Yeah," he says. "Why?"

I remember something Dad said last night. Along with the "Be back by half ten, don't drink, don't talk to strangers" lecture.

"Gran," I groan. "She's here."

"Oh," he says.

"Exactly."

Then Ed is finding me a washcloth to clean my face, a hairbrush, my shoes. Making me coffee and toast and Marmite to take away.

"Thanks," I say.

Ed is standing on the doorstep in last night's T-shirt and boxer shorts. He smiles. "You're welcome."

"I mean it . . . and not just for the toast."

"I know."

And for one brief moment we're us again. Me and Ed. Like we always were. And as I walk down the road, his eyes on my back, I wish I could hold on to them both. Him, and Stella. But it won't work like that. I know I will have to choose.

11

DAD IS waiting for me.

I walk up the bare treads of the stairs. My head's hanging down, heavy with sleep and sun and last night, my stomach alive with butterflies, a can of Coke in my hand to quell them, poison them. I see his feet in front of me, on the landing, faded-brown socks, a hole in the left one. I stop. And wait for the words I know are going to come out. Seen it on the soaps.

"Where the hell have you been?" Like he's scripted.

"Ed's."

"I know that. His mum rang last night. But, why, Jude? You knew your gran was coming."

"I forgot." True. "Where is she?"

"At the beach with Alfie. I've told her you're helping Ed clear out the garage." Lying. To cover for me.

I shrug, like it's nothing. But it's everything. To him.

The TV script starts again. "Have you seen the state of yourself?"

"Yes."

"What's the matter with you lately?"

"Nothing. God, will everyone stop worrying about me? I'm fine — No, I'm better than fine. I'm happy."

"You were drinking . . ."

Mrs. Hickman told him, then. Must have heard Ed carrying me in. "It's just the end of term, Dad. Everyone was out."

Dad looks at the floor, shakes his head. "I can't do this again." But he's talking to himself now. About her, I guess. And I'm sick of it. Of this ghost that stalks us. Unacknowledged. Unspoken. But we both see her, feel her.

I dig my nails into the palms of my hands. "Say it, Dad," I demand. "Say I'm like her. That's what you mean, isn't it? But I'm not. I wish I bloody were. But I'm not."

The words hang there, taunting him. I watch his face, struggling. See what he wants to say bubble up inside him. But he fights it back down.

Eventually his eyes meet mine again. But his face is set now. "Just get washed. They'll be back for lunch at half past."

I laugh. Quick and spiteful. "You are unbelievable." I run up the last stairs, push past him, and slam my bedroom door. Textbook.

I hear him turn the radio on in the kitchen. Radio 2 again. Sunday love songs. I flick on the stereo and press play, not even checking what's loaded. The Rolling Stones reverberate off the walls as I flop down on the bed. Staring at the ceiling. Craving sleep that I know I can't have. I cover my face with my hands and feel a warm wetness. My nails have dug so hard they have drawn blood.

I'm sitting at the dressing table, staring at myself in the mirror. In trousers and a T-shirt now. Last night's dress abandoned on the floor.

People used to say we could be sisters. Me and Mum. Mum would laugh and smile and kiss me. But they were just trying to be nice to her. Just saying the words she wanted to hear. I take after him. Quiet. Plain. A nobody.

Mum was beautiful. Not just like every kid thinks their mum is beautiful. I mean she was like Marilyn and Marlene and Madonna rolled into one. That wild blond hair, eyes an obscure shade of green. Like candied angelica or lime Starburst. Unique. My shooting star, Dad called her. And she was. Lighting up the village for nine years, then burning out. *I am like a low-energy lightbulb,* I think. I laugh at the image in my head. And what is Stella? A Catherine wheel? Maybe a disco ball.

Mum and Dad met in a pub in London. She kept the matchbook in her jewelery box. I have looked at the street on maps. Googled it a hundred times. This once-in-a-lifetime meeting place. The start of it all.

He was at art school in Chelsea, his great escape from Churchtown. She was doing modeling jobs for a hundred pounds and living on her mother's inheritance, her father three years dead. She was in a pop video once. They still show it on MTV, Mum dancing in the background behind some cheesy eighties band with striped T-shirts and blow-dried glam hair.

She said it was love at first sight. Dad would get embarrassed, but I think it was the same for him. When she got pregnant, they thought they would move to France. Live in some stone farmhouse in the South. In lavender fields. Where all artists go, following the light. Him painting, her reading me Keats, teaching me "Frère Jacques."

But then Dad's father died. And Dad had to come back to the farm he'd fought so hard to leave. Gran forbade Mum to follow him. Maybe that's why she did. To spite her. And I was born on the farm in May. A Gemini. Same as her.

Dad says she was like nothing Churchtown had ever seen. She'd walk into the village in Gaultier skirts and stilettos, with me on one hip. She'd send me to school in mismatched wellies or a party dress because she'd lost my shoes or used my skirt to mop up spilled soup. I would get sent home, mortified. But Mum just laughed and let me watch cartoons and made cupcakes.

Those were the good days. On the bad days, I'd come home and she'd still be in bed. Or lying on the sofa in one of Dad's shirts. Eating cornflakes from the box, then lying defiantly in the crumbs. Saying she was too tired to clean. Mrs. Hickman hoovering around her and muttering under her breath.

Highly strung, Gran called it. But I know what she really thought. What everyone thought. And I think of Mental Nigel, sitting outside the launderette, counting red cars and eating candy. And for one brief moment, I'm glad I'm nothing like her.

Mick Jagger has faded into the low electricity hum of the speakers. The back door slams and I hear Alfie's voice singing through the house. Then Gran's restrained, clipped vowels. So different from me and Alfie.

Then Dad.

"Jude!"

"Yeah."

I down the last few mouthfuls of warm, flat Coke and look again at my reflection. Wishing someone else were staring back. But it's still me.

"Jude, darling."

"Hi, Gran."

She kisses me on both cheeks, like the French girl I am not, her lips never once coming into contact with my skin. I can smell soap and coffee and Nina Ricci. Dressed in cream linen, she is immaculate. Out of place in our cramped, mismatched living room.

She isn't staying with us. Now she has the excuse that

there's no room. But even before we moved, she'd find some reason to book a hotel. Said the farm gave her hay fever. "They're cows, not crops," Dad said. But Mum just laughed and said, "Let her waste her money."

"So, you've been helping Edward and his mother."

I feel Dad's eyes on me. Don't-you-daring me. I smile at Gran. "Yes. Sorry I missed you earlier."

"Oh, never mind. We've had a splendid time, haven't we, Alfie?"

"We got ice cream dipped in chocolate, and Gran says I can go to the hotel later and swim in the pool."

"Does she, now?" says Dad.

Gran raises a plucked, arched eyebrow at him that says, *And?*

But Alfie doesn't see it. "It's made of salt water. Did you know that salt actually makes you float? In the Dead Sea you actually float on top of the water because it's, like, so salty."

"I didn't know that, Alfie," says Dad. Lying again. Twice in one morning. Alfie looks pleased. So does Gran. One point for her.

"You must come too, Jude. We can have tea on the lawn."

I hear Stella laugh in my head and force a smile. "Thanks. Maybe." Maybe not.

"So, how were the exams, darling?" Gran perches on the edge of the sofa, tensing in case some neglected spill seeps through her trouser suit. "Have you thought about university yet? Your father tells me Edward is going to King's."

"Give her a chance." Dad glances over at me. "She's only just done her GCSEs."

But Gran ignores that fact. "It pays to think ahead, Tom. You know they have summer programs at Cambridge for less fortunate pupils. To give them a taste. She—"

"She goes to a bloody three-thousand-pounds-a-term girls' school. I'd say she's more than fortunate."

Gran stiffens.

"Dad swore. Dad, you swore." Alfie is delirious with forbidden things.

"Sorry, Alfie . . . Margaret." He nods at Gran.

"I'm only thinking of Jude." Gran holds up her hands.

"I know."

"She has such potential. . . ."

"*She* is in this room," I point out.

But Gran doesn't hear me. Or chooses not to. "And then there's her acting."

"That's a hobby. Not a career."

"That's not what Charlotte thought . . ."

Dad flinches. Mum's name hanging solid between them. Like a swearword. And I think, *She'll stop now; she has to.*

But she doesn't.

". . . not what you used to think. She could have been someone, you know. If—"

"She *was* someone," Dad says deliberately, his face reddening with anger.

84

"Dad," I plead softly. Desperately. "Stop it." I don't want to hear this. Not now. I'm too tired. But he ignores me.

He and Gran blur into one noise. "Don't understand . . . never accepted . . . blame me . . ."

I can't listen anymore. Have to make the noise disappear. "I'm leaving, anyway," I blurt out.

The voices cut out abruptly.

"What?" Dad looks at me, confused.

"I've got an audition. At the Lab. It's a drama school." I pause. "In London."

"Oh, Jude, that's wonderful—" Gran is glowing again. Victorious.

But she hasn't won. Dad plays his trump card. "No," he says.

"What?" It's my turn now.

"You're not going."

"Why?"

"How are you going to pay for it?" he says. "They don't give out grants anymore. How much do you think it costs to go to stage school?"

About three thousand pounds a term, I think. But I don't say it. I don't need to. We all know where the money will come from.

Gran smiles. "You can't keep her here forever, Tom."

Dad drops his head. Then looks up at her. "I'm not trying to. Do you think I want her to end up like me? But she's a kid, Margaret. She's too young. She's too"—he looks over at me, searching for a word—"fragile."

"No, I'm not." I retort. I'm strong. I'm invincible. Like Stella. Aren't I?

But Dad's still going on at Gran. "She needs stability. Normal things. A normal life." He pauses, searching for the words. "Look at what it did to her," he says finally. And he doesn't mean me now. "Those people. Every time she went up to London . . . the state she was in when she got back."

"Because she saw what she was missing," Gran says.

Dad shakes his head. "Because they got her drunk. Gave her—" He stops.

I can feel the tears prick my eyes again and I choke back a sob. But Gran waves her hand. Dismissing it as lies.

Dad turns to me. "I'm sorry, Jude. You're too young."

"I'm sixteen," I cry.

"Exactly. Sixteen. How can you even know what you want to do at this age? Who you want to be?"

I know exactly who I want to be. So does he. And that's what he's scared of. But I don't say that. I use another weapon.

"You did," I spit. "You wanted to be Turner or Whistler or . . . or Monet. What happened to that?"

"Life happened," he says. "And, anyway, I wasn't good enough."

"What if I am, though?"

Dad says nothing. Alfie is crying. Dad tries to pick him up, but he fights and wriggles out of his grip and holds on to my legs. "Don't go." Snot is running down his nose and sticking to my leg. A snail trail.

"It's all right, Alfie," I say, wiping his face. "It's all right."
But it isn't.

Lunch is ham and potatoes, pushed around plates. Only Alfie is really eating. And talking. Back to his endless chattering now. "Did you know that potatoes were the first food grown in space?" Dad clears the table and gets everyone ice cream from the shop freezer. Ice cream. Mum's answer to bad dreams and scraped knees and bee stings. And rows.

I don't go to the hotel with Alfie and Gran. I go back to my room. Back to my bed and the Rolling Stones. Ed calls, but I don't come to the phone. Because it's not him I need now. It's Stella.

But Stella has other plans.

12

IT'S MONDAY. Two days since that night at the Point. Two days since I saw Stella. Gran has gone, Alfie's at school, and Dad and I are working in the shop. Me putting out cans of tuna, boxes of cereal. Him behind the counter, doling out stamps and pensions and explaining passport forms to Mrs. Saunders, who is going to Germany to see her son. "He's got four medals, you know." *And no brain,* I think, *joining the army.*

Mrs. Hickman comes in at noon to do the afternoon shift. "You two not talking?" she huffs.

We are talking. But about nothing. About me spilling tea on the stack of *Daily Mail*s. About whether he should move the tinned peas up a shelf to make more room for olives and stuff for the tourists. The audition doesn't come up. But I know he's thinking about it. We both are.

At lunchtime I walk down to the beach, hoping I'll see her there. Lying in the sun. Blondie on her iPod and a cigarette burning down to her fingers. "Hey, Jude," she'll say. Like nothing's happened. But it has.

I stand on the dunes and scan the shore below me. The beach is busier now. Families from Birmingham, Manchester, Milton Keynes, with kids too young for school. Staying at the holiday park. Or the farm, maybe. Paying cheap prices before the season starts. Surfers with no jobs to go to. No ties. Living in their vans. Just driving from beach to beach, following the tides.

She's not there. But Emily and the Plastics are. In white bikinis. Tiny triangles stretched over their breasts. Legs tanned to perfection. Brazilian waxes making sure nothing shows below the high-cut Lycra. Magazines fighting for towel space with cans of Diet Coke, sun cream, and cigarette packets. An iPod churns out tinny music. Blair is here, somewhere. Out on his board, probably. Emily's head is on his sweatshirt. Staking her claim.

I am in a tank top. One of Stella's. Pink. Tight across my chest. My jeans cut off to the tops of my thighs. Flip-flops that kick sprays of sand up my legs when I walk. Dawce sees me. Says something I can't hear. Emily and the Hollys look up. Eyes hidden behind oversize glasses. I turn quickly to walk away, back to the village, home, but Emily calls my name.

I don't move. It's a trick. Got to be.

"Come here," she shouts.

So I do. Slowly. Picking my way past beach tents and coolers, fat glossy paperbacks, and the colored plastic of buckets and spades and elaborate tennis sets. Then I'm there, in front of them. Not sure why.

"Hi," I say. Like it's a question.

Emily leans back, the sun turning her glasses into mirrors. I can see myself reflected in them. Hands in pockets, uneasy.

She pushes the glasses up. Her eyes are narrow. "So, what was Saturday about?"

Does she mean the drinking? I try to sound casual. "Just overdid it a bit." I try a laugh but it sounds fake. She knows it.

"He's not interested, you know."

And I must look as dumb as I feel. Because she has to spell it out.

"Blair."

I still don't get it. "Interested in what?"

"God, are you stupid?" she snorts. "Anyone. Except me."

"I know," I say. And I mean it.

"So act it."

"But . . ." I'm trying to think. Maybe I did something, said something when I was drunk. But it was Stella he was

90

looking at, not me. Stella who was staring back at him. Wasn't it?

"As if, anyway." Emily pulls back the ring on a Diet Coke. It hisses, and caramel bubbles down the silver and red of the can. She licks it off.

"Is that it?" I wait to be dismissed. Like I've been bad. Told off.

"Mmm-hmm."

The Plastics smile identical smiles at me. Alligator smiles. Not real.

I drop my head and walk away. Not sure where I'm going. Feel their eyes on my back. Hear the laughter, not even stifled. Then I see him. Blair. Wet suit slick with water. Board under his arm. He slows down. His mouth creases up. Like it did at Stella on the Point. "All right, Jude."

I ignore him and keep walking, knowing that Emily is watching.

He laughs. "See you around."

He watches me walk away. I feel his eyes on me. He wants something. That's how people like him choose who to talk to. Sizing up what you can offer. What they can get out of you. Stella, probably. That's what I am. His way to get her.

But I don't know where she is. And I look up at the expanse of sky and pray that my fairy godmother is watching.

13

I'M IN the bathroom, watching Alfie's goldfish floating on its back, eyes glassed over. Dead. Again. Not this one, obviously. But the latest in a long line. All called Harry.

I scoop the fish out of the bowl. It lies stiff in my hand, mouth gaping. Not a real thing anymore. Just scales and fins, its beauty lost forever. I lower my head and breathe in. It smells of old water.

"Flush it."

I swing around and she is standing there. Leaning against the door frame, chewing. Hands fiddling with a hair elastic, pulling it taut, then releasing it. Stella.

"Here." She snaps the elastic and puts it in her pocket. Takes the fish and drops it into the toilet. Pulls the chain.

It swirls around the bowl. A flash of orange against the white. Then it is gone.

I stare at her. Incredulous. Angry. "Where have you been?"

"You sound like your dad."

I do. And I soften. Because she's here now. That's what matters.

"Just . . . I wish you wouldn't do that. Appear out of nowhere."

"Door was open," she says. "You want to be more careful. Anyone could just wander in." She is going through the medicine cabinet, looking for something. "Or maybe you want someone to come in?"

Whatever pill she is searching for, she doesn't find it. She shuts the cabinet and sits on the edge of the bath.

"Like Blair Henderson, for instance." She looks at me, waiting for a reaction.

"What?"

"He likes you. I heard Dawce telling Holly H."

"That's not true. It's you he likes."

Stella shrugs. "Whatever."

So I drop it. Try another tack. "Anyway, what happened the other night? Where did you go?"

"Nothing and nowhere. You got wasted. Which was actually more boring than I thought it would be. So I went home. Just been at the farm since then. Modeling for Dad. I'm meant to be Ophelia. You know, beautiful, but mad."

I smile. "Good casting."

"So, does Tom know yet? About the audition, I mean. Not your colossal incapacity for cheap lager. I assume you threw it back up in here. No way that would get past him."

"At Ed's actually." I grimace.

"Ed's?"

"I slept at his house. . . . On the floor," I add.

But she doesn't ask for details. "So, does your dad know about the Lab?"

"Yeah." I pull at my lip with my teeth. Sigh. "He's not happy."

She shrugs. "None of his business."

"Well . . ." She's right. But it doesn't feel like it.

"He'll come around. Once you're earning top dollar in the West End. Or on TV."

I laugh. Stella fingers the looped cotton of the mat hung over the side of the bath. Pulls a loop out. Then another. Smoker's habit. Always fiddling. Mum did it.

She looks at me, head on one side. "I saw that guy down at the beach last night."

"Who?" I ask.

"Drama bloke."

"Mr. Hughes?"

"Hughsie. That's him."

I see his face in my head. The curl of hair over his collar. Then I see Stella's smile, and I know what's coming.

"Totally tried it on with me."

"Bullshit." But my voice is hesitant. Because I know it isn't.

"Bull true," she confirms. "Anyway, I let him."

Suddenly I am there. On the beach. I hear the cries of the seagulls above the crashing of the waves. Smell the salt on the wind. See Stella reaching out for him, pulling him toward her. Feel his hand hot against her breast. See the desire and fear in his eyes. And the contempt in Stella's as he backs away. Then it's gone. I feel a wave of nausea wash over me. Like it is my shame. My sin.

"Why did you do that?" My voice is slow, stilted.

"Why do you think?" She smiles.

And I realize I know. Have known all along. "Because you can."

"Now you're getting it."

The back door slams. Alfie, back from school.

"That's my cue." Stella stands up.

"Where are you going?" I'm Dad again. Checking up on her. Scared of losing her.

"Just out. Got to see a man about a dog."

"What dog?"

She tuts. "It means stop asking questions."

"Sorry," I murmur. "Come around tomorrow, yeah?"

"Maybe," she says.

I feel the blood drain from my head, and dizziness engulfs me. I clutch at the sink to steady myself. Catch my reflection in the mirror. Pale. Terrified.

Stella sees it and laughs. "God. OK. What are you worried about? I'm not going to run off, if that's what you think."

"I don't," I lie.

"You don't get it, do you?" She stands behind me. Puts her arms around me. I meet her eyes in the glass. Her easy smile gone now. "We need each other," she says. "We're soul mates. Like that Greek philosophy thing—with the two halves of the egg waiting to meet each other."

"Aristotle," I say.

"Whatever. We're Bonnie and Clyde." She smiles again.

"Laurel and Hardy?" I try.

"Morecambe and Wise."

"Fred and Ginger." We're both laughing now. Stella's face next to mine. Her hair falling down over my chest.

"I'll always come back," she says.

And I see the way she looks at me, feel the way she is holding me. And this time, I believe her.

"Where's Harry?" Alfie is in the kitchen. Empty fishbowl in his hands, water slopping out over the floor.

Dad is sliding something frozen out of a packet onto a baking tray. He looks up and sees the bowl. Then looks at me. Realizes what I have done. What Stella has done. But I don't care. I'm tired of pretending. He's not five years old anymore. And it's not like she killed it. They die. Everything dies eventually.

Alfie asks again. "Dad?"

But I answer. "He's gone," I say.

Alfie looks at me. Then back at Dad. Expectantly. Waiting for him to deny it. But he doesn't.

"Alfie . . ."

"Where is he?" Alfie demands.

"I flushed him," I say. "He was already dead. I said a prayer and everything," I lie.

Alfie drops the bowl. The glass smashes on the hard tiles and I feel water and colored gravel splash across my bare feet.

"Oh, Alfie . . . Don't move." Dad grabs the mop.

"I'm sorry," I say.

But Alfie is crying. And then Dad is hugging him. Telling him it'll be all right. That Harry was just old. That he can choose another fish tomorrow.

I kneel down in the dirty water and pick up the pieces of glass, all the time thinking, *It's only a bloody goldfish.* But not saying it. Because no one ever does around here.

That night I'm woken by the sound of something falling on the kitchen floor, rolling along the ridged surface. Then footsteps, heavy, the knock and scrape of a chair. I squint at the glowing red numbers on the alarm clock, my eyelids aching with sleep and the heat. It's past one. I hear a clink. The sound of glass against glass. I sit bolt upright. Stella. It can only be her. What is she doing? What if Dad catches her?

Sweat sticks my feet to the painted boards of the landing. Dad's bedroom door is shut. "Don't wake up," I beg. "Please don't wake up."

I hear a thud. Then something else. Something slammed hard on the table. Oh, Stella, Stella.

But it's not her. It's him. Dad. He's sitting at the table, his head resting on his hands. Bottle of shop whiskey open. An inch of it in the glass in front of him. I realize he's drunk, and I want to go back. To hide. Don't want to see him like this. But it's too late. He raises his head and looks straight at me, in my T-shirt and knickers, framed by the door.

"Jude." It's a strangled sound, a sort of sob. "Oh, Jude, I'm sorry," he says. "I—"

"It doesn't matter," I say quickly, trying to shut him up. I want to get out, before he says anything else, but he won't let me.

"It does." He shakes his head.

I should go to him, I think. Sit with him. Let him say all that stuff. Tell him it's not his fault. Any of it. That I'm sorry. That I miss her too. But something about the way he is makes me shrink back. His face is contorted. By drink. Or sorrow. He's not real. Not him. I stay in the doorway, my arms wrapped tight around myself for protection.

"You can go," he says. "To London. I won't stop you."

I nod.

"Just promise me you'll—" He sobs again, stifling it with the back of his hand. "Just be careful, Jude."

98

"I will," I whisper.

His hands are over his mouth, elbows on the table. He's staring at me. But it's like he's seeing someone else.

"You look—"

Say it, I think. *Just say it.*

But he can't. And in that second I feel nothing but pity and hatred for the pathetic wreck sitting in front of me. This shell of a man who can only speak when he's drunk. Who has made me the shadow that I am.

"Go to bed, Dad." I spit the words out, hard with contempt.

He nods. But his hand falls to clutch the glass again.

I lie in bed, the heat enveloping me, taking me with it. "You should be happy," Stella says. The Stella in my head. "You've gotten what you wanted."

But I haven't. Not at all.

14

July

THE HEAT is unbearable. Headlining the *Western Daily* and every conversation at the till. Scorching the grass brown. Steering wheels burn to the touch, and passengers' faces drip with sweat, windows wound down and Atlantic FM blaring out.

Stella and I lie on the Point, wearing SPF 30, smoking and reading lines. All the time, me trying to forget why we're there. The audition. Pretend it's nothing. But it overwhelms my every thought.

It's just a day away now. I've booked the train. Dad paid for it. He has given me a map, an A–Z with the Tube stop and the Lab marked in red pen.

Sometimes I'm scared of getting in. Scared that London

is bigger, brighter, better than I can ever be. That I won't touch its surface. That it will swallow me and spit me out. Another small-town nobody who didn't make it.

Other times I'm scared I won't get in. That I'm nowhere near good enough. That Isabella sounds like a whining prissy, or an overblown stage-school brat. That I should have picked Juliet after all. Or Viola, and gone for laughs. That the piece is too obscure. That I can't dance. That I'll end up like the other village kids, doling out gum and papers and getting fat, purple veins bulging on my legs like Mrs. Hickman's.

"Christ. It's like Calcutta out here." Stella drops the book and picks up her cigarettes. A bead of sweat runs down her chest, bikini top discarded for a lineless tan.

"Kolkata. It got changed. Anyway, come on. It's tomorrow."

"For God's sake. You've done the same speech for weeks. Even I know it by heart. *That had he twenty heads to tender down/On twenty bloody blocks, he'd yield them up . . .* Fol de rol, blah blah—"

"OK!"

She shrugs and lights up, holding the packet out to me. I take one and reach into my pocket for a lighter. Not her Zippo. A red plastic one, from the shop, that Stella said I needed now that I was serious. I am, I guess. My throat and lungs slowly hardening to the harsh burning. And I crave them. Not the nicotine, maybe. Not yet. But the feeling I get watching myself being this person.

101

"You need to look different." Stella brushes ash off her left breast. "There's no shock. You're a nun playing a nun. You need to look like—I don't know—like a slut."

I smile. "Like you, you mean."

"Ouch. But, yeah," she concedes. "Then when you start doing the whole *Isabella, live chaste* thing, it's, like, oh, my God."

"I guess," I admit.

"And drama students are all sluts anyway." Stella inhales again, then speaks through the smoke. "So, if you're a slut that can play a nun, you're their ideal candidate."

"I'm not, though," I insist.

"They don't know that." She smiles.

I shiver, despite the heat. I'm scared. Because I know what Stella's makeovers involve. Seen my Barbie and others like it go from prom queen to Goth whore.

Stella leans back on her elbows, smoke mixing with her laughter. "Don't worry. I won't make you look like a freak." She smiles, waiting for the beat. "Not totally, anyway."

I laugh and kick her. She kicks me back. Then I pick up the Shakespeare and hit her with it.

"Bitch!" Leaving her cigarette in her mouth, she grabs her Coke and tips it over me. It soaks through my T-shirt, making it stick to my hot skin.

I yelp. "Stella! That's gross."

"Take it off," she tells me.

"I can't. I'm not wearing a bra."

"So? Not like I haven't seen it before."

"I know, but—"

"But nothing. Who else is up here? A load of random tourists? They won't give a toss."

The top stuck to me, I look like a photo in a girlie magazine anyway. I pull it over my head, then pour the last of my water over me.

"What are you doing?" Stella says.

"Wasps." Like it's obvious.

"Great. So we'll die of thirst now." She sighs, then smiles at me slyly. "Wasp stings might improve them, anyway."

"Stella!" I hug my chest, embarrassed.

"Joking. You're gorgeous and you know it."

I smile. "You know the Hollys are getting theirs done for their eighteenth birthdays—34DD."

"How low-rent." Stella lies back and closes her eyes behind the Ray-Bans. I lie next to her, her arm against mine. She reaches for my hand and squeezes it. I feel safe and warm. And that's how we fall asleep.

"Jude?"

I open my eyes. Everywhere is white. Sun-bleached. I close them again. The sky is burned onto my retina.

"Jude?"

I sit up. Stella is gone. Ed is standing over me. Staring. I grab the damp T-shirt and clutch it to me. I feel anger rise in me. That she's gone. That he's here. I don't know.

"Had a good look, have you?" I sneer. "How long have you been there anyway?"

"What do you think I am? Some kind of perv? You're just a schoolgirl." He picks up the bikini top Stella has left and throws it at me. "Here. You never know who might be watching." His sarcasm bites me.

I feel anger coursing through me. Electricity, making my heart pound, the blood singing in my head. But I put it on, pulling the red halter neck over my head, snapping the strap. "What are you doing here, anyway?" I ask.

"Came to find you. It's tomorrow, isn't it? The audition?"

I pick up the half-smoked cigarette and fumble for my lighter. "Yup."

"So . . . good luck," he says.

I exhale slowly. Shrug. "Thanks."

Ed is silent. And it is a silence I can feel. Not like our old ones. Awkward now. And I don't know if it's just Stella. Or if there's something else, something changing us, pushing us apart.

"Good luck," he repeats.

"You said that."

"Yeah."

Silence.

"What time do you get back?" he asks.

"Dunno. Half nine."

Silence.

"I'll pick you up from the station."

"Dad'll be there," I retort.

"So he's changed his mind?"

"Yup."

Silence.

"That's good."

I shrug and say nothing still. Though he's right.

"Jude. You can . . . talk to me, you know. If something's wrong."

"What are you now, a shrink?"

"No. God. It's just. You're not—I don't know—*you* anymore, Jude."

I laugh, spiteful. "Who am I, then?"

"I don't know."

Silence.

"Well. Call me." He stands up, one hand shielding his eyes against the sun. "Tell me how it goes."

"Yup."

Silence. I can feel the cigarette burning down, the ash falling on my fingers.

"See you, then."

"Wouldn't want to be you." But I'm not smiling this time. Because I mean it.

"Whatever." Ed shakes his head.

I watch him walk back up the slope to the Land Rover. Slow in the heat. And the anger still burns inside me. I'm not a schoolgirl. Not anymore. And I'm going to prove it.

I decide I'll let Stella do what she wants. Be her personal *Extreme Makeover* project. From nobody to smoking hot in one edit.

*   *   *

Stella shows up after tea. Takes the new *Vogue* and *Elle* off the shelf downstairs and sets up a salon in my bedroom. Cheesy music on the CD player and my head wrapped in a fading pink towel as we flick through the glossy pages for an hour. Peroxide mixing with the sickly sweet rock-candy smell of nail varnish. Dizzy. High. The heat slowing everything down. Waiting for me to emerge.

Five hours later and I'm staring at the not me in the mirror. I am different. Four-packets-of-Clairol-Ash-Blond, heavy-black-eyeliner, and lipstick different. Not obscure anymore, but stand-out, look-at-me bright. Shimmering. A butterfly.

"I can't believe it's me."

"You. Totally. Rock." Stella nudges me over on the chair so she can squeeze in next to me. We see our reflections and laugh. Because I'm not me. I'm her.

She leans on my shoulder. "There is no me without you. Remember?"

We look at ourselves. At each other.

"See, Jude?"

And I do see. I am still me inside. But now I have Stella's hair, Stella's face. She is everything I am not. Everything I want to be. And I can feel it. Feel what she must feel every day. Feel what Mum must have felt. Because right then I know that the world turns for me alone.

I go downstairs for Diet Coke. Dad is in the kitchen, reading the sports pages. He looks up, startled. I wait for the shouting and the demands to dye it back. Back to brown. Back to nothing. But he just stares at the stranger I am now, then goes back to who beat who and by how much. As if it matters. As if it makes a difference.

I walk back up the stairs. Slowly. Each footstep digging into him, I think. Reminding him of life.

15

"YOU LOOK like a film star." Alfie is agog. His Rice Krispies stopped snap, crackle, and popping ten minutes ago and lie soggy in the milk.

I am trying to chew toast. But the butter clags in my mouth and my stomach contracts, full of nerves. I drop it onto the plate and push it away.

"Dad, can I have yellow hair too?" Alfie dreams of another new disguise.

"It's not yellow; it's blond," I mutter.

"No, you can't," Dad says, handing him a glass of juice. He gives me a foil package. "I've made you a sandwich for the train. Here."

I can smell sausages. Last night's tea. Cold with

ketchup on sliced white, I guess. My stomach turns. But I know it's a big thing. That he's trying to make up for before. "Thanks." I push the package into my bag. Where I know it'll lie forgotten, heating up before I throw it in a bin on a London street.

I'm wearing another dress from Dixie's, bought with the last of Gran's money. A green vintage thing with a sweetheart neckline. And scuffed red ballet flats. All Stella's work. Said they made me look interesting but not like I was trying too hard. "Everyone else'll be in black. Bloody drama students always are. You'll stand out. In a good way."

But alone I feel odd. Not me but not her either. Just a stupid girl dressing up in someone else's clothes. And I want to go back upstairs and put something black on, so I am one of them.

"Oh, my Lord!"

Mrs. Hickman is here to look after Alfie and the shop while Dad takes me to the train. A blur of white flesh and blue cotton and a faint smell of bleach.

She stares at my head.

"You let her do that?"

Dad holds his hands up.

Mrs. Hickman shakes her head. "Jude, you had lovely hair. Why, for pity's sake?"

Sarcasm rises like bile. I smile. A film-star smile. "Because I'm worth it."

Alfie giggles.

But Dad saves me. And himself. "Jude. Time to go."

I grab my bag and push back the chair, scraping the tiles and knocking the table. Alfie's juice spills.

"Dad!" Alfie is soaked, the orange staining his pajamas.

"Jude." Dad groans.

"Sorry." I sigh.

But Mrs. Hickman already has a cloth. She must carry them in her handbag. Maybe mums do that. Normal mums. She mops the table and sends Alfie upstairs to change.

"Well, good luck. Though why you lot all want to go up to London I'll never know."

She sounds like a sitcom character. The dumb local. And I'm the surly teenager with big ideas, set for a fall.

"Because it's not here," I say.

She tuts and tips my uneaten toast in the bin.

Dad stays in the van, waiting until the train has pulled out. I watch through the window. See him start up and turn left back to the coast road. Feel the ten-pound note he pushed into my hand before I got out. "Just in case," he said.

"I've got money," I lied. But I took it anyway. Put it in my purse with the twenty-pence coins he'd taken out of the till and given me for phone calls. I don't have a mobile. No point. Churchtown is the Wild West. The last outpost with no reception. So the phone box is always busy. Tourists queuing in the summer to order cabs and pizza and check surf reports. Saying, "Isn't it a relief to be away from it all?" Like it was in the seventies. But secretly longing to get back to their BlackBerrys and Wi-Fi and lattes.

The train is quiet. Just six other seats taken in my carriage. The rest reserved from Exeter, Taunton, Reading. Places that sound gray, lifeless. Nowhere places. I look at the other passengers, with their newspapers and polystyrene cups and early morning silence. All men, four in suits. Not even the heat can persuade them out of their uniform. Two older. Retired, maybe. Still smart, though. I wonder why they are on the train. Are they going somewhere life-changing, like me? Or just to work, one of the faceless, nameless thousands scuttling into tall buildings before scuttling home again. Never making their mark. Never leaving their imprint on the world.

The Lab dances inside me. Turning my stomach, making my foot tap and my hand shake, alive with nerves. And I wish Stella were here.

"You won't need me," she'd said, pushing me at the mirror again. "Look. I'm with you. I'm in you."

But I want her next to me. Telling me it's all right. That I can do it. That I'm special.

"Can't afford it," she said.

"I'll lend it to you, then."

But she shook her head. "You'll be fine."

I say it to myself. I'll be fine. I'll be fine. If I say it enough, maybe it will come true.

I take the sandwich out of my bag and drop it in the plastic bin between the seats. One of the men looks up. Because of the smell, perhaps. A meaty, breakfast smell.

He catches my eye and looks away again. Back to the *Telegraph*. Some story about National Health Service budgets. Probably does this journey every day. Sits in the same seat. Has the same cup of coffee and the same apple. The same conversation with the conductor. I close my eyes and lean my head against the windowpane. Feeling the rocking of the train. *I am never going to be stuck,* I think. I want every day to be different. To surprise me.

Today it does.

"There you are."

I jolt up.

She crashes down opposite me, spreading herself over two seats.

"Stella?" Relief washes over me.

"No, the Queen of Sheba," she retorts.

"But . . . what are you doing?"

"Coming with you, duh." She pulls out her makeup bag and spills the contents across the Formica tabletop.

"I thought you didn't have the money."

"Don't. I'll hide in the loo when the conductor comes." She flicks open a gold compact and studies herself. "Urgh. I look like death. This is entirely too early."

She clicks it shut.

I glance across at *Telegraph* Man, to see if he is watching her circus. But she is invisible. We both are.

"So, Tom dropped you off. Did he wish you bad luck?"

"Yeah—no, I mean . . . I didn't see you at the station."

"Toilets. Desperate for a pee. Too much coffee. God, Jude. You're worse than Mrs. Hickman with the twenty questions. I wouldn't have bothered if I'd known I was going to get the Spanish Inquisition."

"Sorry. It's just that . . . I thought I was on my own."

"That can be arranged. I'll get off at Hicksville or wherever the next station is."

"No, don't," I blurt out, not caring about the desperation that I know she can hear in every syllable. "I want you here."

"Good. I'm gasping for a ciggy." Stella shakes her bag on the table. Three packets of cigarettes fall out. She does her trick, flicking the packet and pulling one out with her lips. *Telegraph* Man coughs and points at the NO SMOKING stickers plastered over every window.

Stella takes the cigarette out of her mouth. "Christ. Keep your hair on." She tucks the packet under her bra strap. "I'll go to the toilets, then, or hang out the window or something." She stands up and looks at me. "Coming?"

I shake my head. It's too early for me, still.

"Suit yourself. Want anything from the dining car?"

"Coke. Full fat. I need the energy."

"Got any cash?"

"Oh. Yeah." I find my purse. Hand her Dad's tenner.

"Thanks. I'll keep the change."

I watch as she walks up the carriage, the suits turning to look at her, like she knew they would. *She is incredible,*

I think. I open her compact and look at myself. And I smile. Because, for once, I feel a bit incredible too.

The train stops at Plymouth. *Telegraph* Man gets off, along with two of the others. The station is packed with daytrippers. Going to London to see the sights. The British Museum. Buckingham Palace. Madame Tussauds. Stuff I saw when I was a kid. Mum would take me, and I'd come home with plastic Beefeaters, police helmets, snow globes with a red London bus and the Houses of Parliament inside.

Stella is still not back.

"Are these seats taken?"

I look up. A woman with a boy, smaller than Alfie. Too young for school. The woman is nodding at Stella's seat. Seats.

"Yes."

She glares at me. Like I'm lying.

"She went to the dining car," I say, like it's obvious.

The woman grabs the boy's hand and pulls him to the cramped airline seats behind us. And I go back to staring out the window.

The conductor comes around to check tickets.

"Someone sitting here?" He is looking at Stella's seat. At her makeup strewn across the table.

I shake my head. "Nope."

He nods and moves on.

I hear the woman behind me snort. But I don't care what she thinks. I just want Stella to come back.

She does. Eventually. Somewhere between Taunton and Westbury. Smelling of alcohol. Vodka and Coke. It is ten in the morning. Too early to serve. She must have brought it with her. Poured it into the can.

"What happened?" I ask.

Her face shines with a secret. "If I told you, I'd have to kill you."

"Stella. Come on."

I know it is going to be a man before she says it.

"Bloke in first class. Asked him for a light outside the toilet. Next thing he's in there with me, and it's not a pee he's after."

"That is gross."

She shrugs.

I shake my head. "You are so full of it."

"Maybe." She smiles. "Maybe not. Guess you'll never know. . . . Oh, yeah." She opens her bag and pulls out a can of Coke. "I forgot. This is for you."

"Thanks." It's warm, but I open it anyway. It hisses, spurting over the side and onto the table.

"Shit." I mop it away with my hand, steering it toward the floor.

The woman behind me leans around the seat. "Do you mind?"

Stella stares at her. "No. Obviously not."

The woman darts back. Unsure what to do or say next. So she does nothing. Like I knew she would. You don't argue with Stella.

Stella picks up a discarded newspaper from across the aisle and presses it down on the Coke.

"Thanks."

"All rubbish anyway. Best thing for it." She smiles as she drops it in the bin on top of the sandwich. The smell of cooked meat wafts up again.

The train is hurtling through nameless small towns, station signs illegible, everything blurring into one endless redbrick-and-hanging-basket ribbon.

Stella opens a packet of Jaffa Cakes, the chocolate melting on her fingers. She licks it off, then offers me one. I take it, the artificial orange taste stinging my tongue. Stella smiles. "Who'd you rather . . . ?"

We play for an hour. Then we fall asleep in the dull throbbing heat of the home counties.

I wake up an hour later. Stella is still pressed against the window, sleeping off the vodka.

Outside, the flowers and *Railway Children* station houses are gone, replaced by apartments and office blocks. Mosques and church spires pierce the hazy blue sky, competing for space with tinted glass skyscrapers. A pink neon clock a meter wide and twenty meters up tells me it is 12:13 and 29°C. I can hear sirens and the sound of horns and shouting. Life.

I stare, like a child seeing the city for the first time. Seeing the brilliance and light and wonder.

"Where are we?" Stella sits up and rubs an eye, pushing mascara across her cheek in a wide arc.

I reach over and wipe it off for her. "London."

16

WE ARE sitting on railings outside the Tube station. Two hours to kill before the audition, we're bathing in the sunshine after the dark heat and sweat of the underground. I light up a cigarette, trying to drug the butterflies, calm them down, and watch the world rush past like sped-up movie film. Skinny girls in heels carrying Urban Outfitters bags. Cabdrivers laughing at some dirty joke. People everywhere, the Tube spewing another hundred out every few minutes and swallowing a hundred more. Human traffic.

I try to imagine Dad here. Dad with the smell of cow and hay on him. Dad who still wears his checkered shirts and cable-knit jumpers in the shop. I try to see him in the crowd, one of them. With the same purpose, the same ease. But all I can see is the man who gave up on it. Who went back to the farm. Whose paintings got boxed up and lost in the attic chaos of old toys and unwanted clothes. I remember him that night at the table. Drunk. And I swear I will never be like him. "This is me," I say to the crowds. To the shops, to the cars bumper to bumper on the melting asphalt. "This is me."

"What?" Stella flicks ash onto the taxi parked beside us. "I could murder a drink. There must be a pub near here."

"Stell—"

"Come on." She drops her cigarette on the pavement. Stubs it out with studied elegance. "Steady the nerves."

"OK. Fine. But just one, yeah?" Still the old Jude, somewhere in there.

"Whatever."

"Vodka and Coke. Twice." Stella pulls out her cigarettes.

"No smoking, love." The barman. Australian.

"Jesus." Stella drops her bag on the zinc surface, the buckle clanking against the shiny metal. "Anyone would think it was bad for you."

"Did you mean double vodka and double Coke or just double vodka?" The barman is holding a single glass up.

"No, duh. Two vodkas. Two Cokes. Two glasses."

He shrugs and does as he's told, squirting premix cola into the alcohol.

"Not even real Coke," sighs Stella, world-weary at sixteen. "Whatever happened to the good old days?"

But I'm not really listening. I'm thinking of her. Of Mum in the pub, that day, somewhere near here. She said she'd danced on the bar to David Bowie. I look around me. At the Habitat paper lanterns, the polished floor. I feel a loss. An emptiness. Like I need more. I need to see chandeliers, a jukebox, a wooden bar, pitted with stiletto heels. Not this cold metal in front of me. I want to sit on the same cracked leather that she did. I want to pee in the same cramped space. I want to know what it felt like to be her. But instead I just feel like me. Jude. Pretending again.

"Here. Drink up." Stella pushes one of the vodkas to me.

I take it and gulp it down. It burns my throat and the bubbles sting, making me cough.

"Bloody hell." Stella is impressed. "Here. You need it more than me." She pushes the second glass over. I drink. Slower this time. Letting it take over. Seep into me. I know I shouldn't. Know it's stupid. But I want to feel something. Anything but the fear and self-loathing I am full of right now.

"Got any money left?" I ask.

Stella stares at me, unsmiling. "No. Not for drink, anyway."

"It's mine," I protest. "Dad gave it to me."

"Bollocks. You still owe me, remember?" She stands up. "Anyway, party's over. You need to eat. Curtain's up in half an hour."

"When did you get all Mother Superior?" I whine.

"After the third vodka," she replies. "Come on, Jude. This is your chance to get away. And you're blowing it."

"'Kay . . . shit." I slip off the bar stool and lurch into Stella.

She grabs my arm. "Out. Now."

I drag my bag off the bar, knocking a glass to the floor. It shatters on the stripped wood and spatters my shoes as I am marched to the door, James Blunt singing, *You're beautiful* . . . I laugh at the irony. And stumble out into the sobering sun.

"Are you sure this is right?" I ask, panic marking my voice.

We have been walking for twenty minutes, Stella in charge of the A–Z. The shops have given way to stucco terraces, with window boxes half camouflaging security bars and Porsches parked outside. I am sweating into the dress. Dark patches ring my underarms. Vodka on my breath. I'm a mess.

"'Course it bloody is," she snaps. "Don't you trust me?" Stella throws the A–Z at me and it falls to the ground. I stoop to pick it up, but she keeps walking, knowing I will run to catch her. I do. And link my arm into hers. But she shrugs me off.

"Just wait, Stella. Please stop." I am trying to walk and read the map at the same time.

"Christ, Jude." Stella is angry. With me. With us. I don't know.

"I'm sorry," I say. "Please. I just lost it. I'm scared."

She stops, rolls her eyes. "Here . . ." She holds out her hand for the map. I pass it to her.

"Gloucester Road. See?" She points to a yellow line. One in thousands that mean nothing to me. Bear no resemblance to the street I am standing in. "That's where we are. The Lab is here." She points to a thinner white line, just a few millimeters away. She was right all along. She doesn't need to say it. Just links my arm in hers and pulls me forward. "And don't beg. Ever. It's demeaning."

"I'm sorry," I say.

"And stop saying sorry."

"Sorry."

The *A–Z* hits me in the chest and I laugh. Because I know we're OK. Me and her. And I thank God, or who-ever, that she is there. Because with her I stand a chance. With her I can do anything. Be anybody. Be somebody.

17

"TOTO, I'VE a feeling we're not in Kansas anymore."

Stella is right. This is as far from backyard, small town, redneck as it gets. The Lab. The lobby is like a scene from *Fame*. Rows of black-and-white head shots of people I recognize from TV. Catlike girls in leg warmers holding packets of cigarettes, leaning against the walls or stretching on the floor. First or second years. They all know one another, looking up when Stella and I crash through the door. Deciding who I am. What I am. I know what they're thinking. Not even trailer-trash cool. I'm Anne of Green Gables. Wholesome. Country. I look down at my red shoes. I'm Dorothy.

"It's like we've died and gone to hell. Or Abercrombie and Fitch." Stella is shaking her head.

I poke her in the ribs.

"What? They're a bunch of plastics. You're way better than any of them."

"Yeah, right."

"God, Jude. Now is not the time to go all wallflower on me."

But I feel weird. Maybe it's just the king-size Snickers and two packets of crisps Stella forced me to eat on the way. I need to pee as well. Three vodka and Cokes and two bottles of Evian are demanding to be let out.

Stella glances at me. "Has to be said, you do look like shit."

"Thanks."

"Anytime." She smiles.

"I need the loo."

"In a minute. Come on."

She marches me to the front desk. Stella does the talking.

"Hi. Jude Polmear. Two o'clock."

The receptionist is all tight bun, tight mouth, and Joan Crawford makeup. A fading fifty-year-old. She's thinking the same as the others as she types my name into the computer. No chance. I am one of thirty for three places. I want to go home. I tug at Stella's arm but she pushes me away.

Joan Crawford speaks. "Down the corridor. Wait on the chairs on the left. You'll be called."

"Toilets?" I ask.

She points down the same corridor.

"Thanks so much," says Stella. And then, "Witch!" under her breath, still smiling.

"Come on." I am desperate now.

"OK." Stella links arms again as we walk quickly down the corridor. "What's she on, anyway? Anyone would think someone had appointed her Simon bloody Cowell."

She kicks the bathroom door open.

The Lab may be all Norman Foster glass and chrome, but the toilets are regulation dive. Smell of bleach drowning out the filth and smoke. Lipstick messages on the walls. Tampons spilling out of the sanitary bins.

I lock myself in a stall and pee for what seems like an eternity, nerves eased by the sweet relief of it.

But as I pull my knickers up, I feel a wave of sickness wash over me and I drop onto my knees, staring my pee in the face. I retch but nothing comes up.

Stella bangs on the door.

"Bulimia is so last year."

"Vodka." I retch again, trying to heave something up. But it won't come.

"You only had three," she says. "You need to work on your alcohol capacity."

The nausea subsides. I flush the toilet and open the door.

"Maybe it's nerves." I turn on a tap and splash lukewarm water on my face. I don't feel any better.

"Whatever. Get over it."

"Thanks for the sympathy."

She smiles. Looks at me staring at myself in the graffitied mirror. "Well, you may not look like a nun, but you're giving good turmoil. Very Isabella."

I want to smile, but I can't. My head is full of the wrong things. I try to pull Isabella's lines out of the chaos, but they won't come.

"I can't do it, Stell."

"What?"

"The audition. I'm not doing it. I can't even remember my lines."

"You can. *That had he twenty heads to tender down/On twenty bloody blocks, he'ld yield them up.*"

I shake my head.

"Come on. This is what you want, Jude. Don't wimp out on me now. Don't be him. Don't be Tom."

But tears are rolling down my cheeks, taking the mascara with them. Washing away the disguise.

"Right. I'll do it, then," she says.

I look up. "What?"

"If you won't go in, I will."

I don't understand. "But you can't . . . you don't have an audition."

"No. But you do."

And I realize what she's saying. What she's going to do. For me. And I love her. For caring. For daring to.

But it's wrong. It can't work. I shake my head. "They'll suss it."

"How? No one knows what you look like yet."

"What if I—if you get in? They take photos in there."

"So? Same hair. Same clothes." She pulls me to the mirror. "Look. I'm you." And then she starts to sing. But it's not her voice; it's mine. It's eerie. Like watching a better, more brilliant, version of myself. Like the camera on my life has focused and suddenly I'm clear.

I shiver and look away. "You can't."

"Just watch me." She smiles at herself in the mirror and shakes her hair back over her shoulders. "I'm Jude, and I'm fabulous."

The door opens and a man sticks his head around.

"Oh, sorry. Jude Polmear? Two o' clock?"

I open my mouth but Stella's voice rings out. "Yes, that's me."

"You're next." He nods.

"Coming." She smiles.

The door closes.

"You see?" She hands me her bag.

"You don't have to do this," I say.

"Yes, I do," she replies. And I know she's right. Because I can't. Because it's my only way out. My last hope. Or I will suffocate. Like him.

"So, how do I look?" she asks. But she knows the answer.

"You look amazing." And she does. She is beautiful. A star. How could they not want her?

"Great. Because I am so ready for my close-up."

And she is gone.

* * *

I sit on a plastic chair in the corridor. The audition room is on another floor, but somehow I can still hear her. Or me. Hear her speaking the words I have spent months learning, practicing. Feel the gaze of the panel on her, watching the way she moves. The way Isabella moves. See them nod and take notes. See an older woman whisper something to a young guy with sideburns. He smiles, his eyes never moving from her face. From Stella. Maybe I am remembering a scene from a film. The girl from nowhere, rocking their world. Whatever it is, I am in the room with Stella. I can see they want her. And I wish it were me. I wish it were me.

Stella is breathless, face flushed. I have never seen her like this. Not cool. Not above it.

"You are *so* in," she says as she pulls me off the chair.

"Stella, shut up!" I look around, worried someone is listening.

"What?" She grabs my arm and runs, leading me to the lobby. "Jude Polmear is a star!" she shrieks.

People watch as we fly out the doors. I am laughing now, breathless too. It is infectious. I pull Stella down the steps. "What did they say?"

"I was awesome. Well, you were. Your Isabella was"—she searches for the word—"touched. That's what Ben said, anyway."

"Ben?"

"Head of first year. Thirty-something. Rockabilly side-burns. Cute, really, if you like that kind of thing. Which you probably do." She takes her cigarettes out of her bag, lights two, and hands one to me. "Totally fancies you, by the way."

I inhale, then blow the smoke out slowly. And laugh. "Oh, my God."

"Absolutely." Stella grins.

"What else did he say?"

"That you're a bit nerdy but they can beat that out of you."

"Ha, ha. Come on. What?"

Stella shrugs. "Nothing, really. Just that you'd hear in a few weeks. But you're in. I could tell. You're in, Jude!"

And I want to be happy. I do. But . . . "What if they find out? About you, I mean."

"They won't." She stubs her cigarette out on the chrome *L* of the Lab sign.

And she is so definite, so full of conviction, in herself, in me, that right here, right now, I believe her.

The train runs slowly. Signal failure at Newbury. Seven hours of sweaty commuter-packed hell. I sleep. God knows what Stella does. It is past ten when we get back.

Stella hugs me on the platform. "Remember me when you're famous."

"Totally. I'll send you a Christmas card," I joke.

She pulls back and looks at me. Her face has changed. Not laughing now. "I mean it."

"As if I'd forget you," I say.

She keeps staring. Then her face relaxes and she is Stella again. "So. I'm off like a dirty sock."

"Wait. Don't you want a lift?"

"What, with lover boy?" She nods at the car park.

I look. It's Ed. I scan the parking lot for Dad's van. But it's not there. Just a couple of minivans. Wives picking up late husbands. *Ed must have called him,* I think. *Offered to do it.*

"Oh."

"Exactly. Have fun."

"But . . . what are you going to do?"

"Dunno. Hitch. Call my dad. I have my contacts." She shrugs.

"Are you sure?"

"God. Just go, will you?" She rolls her eyes.

"OK, I'm going. But he's not my lover boy."

"Whatever." She laughs.

"I mean it," I say. And I do. Ed is Ed. I look at him again, leaning against the Land Rover. He waves. I raise my hand. "Stell, I—"

"Like I said, whatever."

"See you tomorrow, then?" She is already walking away. I call after her. "Not if I see you first, right?"

"Now you're getting it."

And she doesn't look back. But I know she is smiling. I can feel it radiate out, seeping into me. And I keep it there as I cross the car park to meet Ed, like a piece of Stella inside me, ready to answer his hundred questions. Not caring that they will be lies. Because Stella is right. I am a star.

18

ALFIE HAS a new fish. A black one this time, called Jude. Named in my honor, apparently, for when I go away. Harry long forgotten. I am watching her circle endlessly around her bowl as I eat toast with peanut butter. It is three days since the audition. Dad hasn't said much, just asked if it went OK. Alfie is full of questions, though. Did I see anyone famous? Did anyone try to mug me? Were there terrorists on the Tube? I say yes to all of them. He is delighted.

Jude, the other Jude, surfaces. Gulping at the air. I wonder how long she will last.

"That your breakfast?" Mrs. Hickman pushes past me on her way to the kettle.

I look at the clock on the kitchen wall. It is half ten. I shrug. "Yeah. So?"

"You could always give me a hand on the till, you know." She smiles. Trying to needle me. Like she's always done. But I don't need needling now. I have Stella.

"Thanks but . . . no." I swill back a glass of orange juice and stand up. "See you."

"Put them in the sink, will you, love?"

I stare at her. Then say it. Words I've heard on the telly. Have toyed with for years. "You're not my mother. You don't even live here."

Mrs. Hickman stops. Then shakes her head, wondering what happened to nice sweet little Jude. Jude who helped her make jam tarts and Christmas crackers. Jude who never answered back, who never swore, who never got drunk and threw up in her bathroom.

She's not here right now, I want to say. She has left the building.

I pick up the plate and glass and clatter them into the sink, hearing the chink of breaking glass.

"Jude," Mrs. Hickman protests.

I ignore her and go back upstairs to wait for Stella.

She smells of salt and smoke and suntan lotion when she arrives, crashing down next to me on the bed, the sand in her hair covering my sheets with a fine layer of grit.

"Stell!" I brush it onto the fading carpet.

"Sorry. Occupational hazard."

"What time is it?"

"I don't know." She shrugs. "Four, maybe."

I wonder where the hours have gone. Don't remember falling asleep.

"Where have you been?"

"Duh. Beach."

"Why didn't you call for me?"

"So. I'm calling for you now." She lights up a cigarette. Her tenth of the day, judging by the half-empty packet. "Don't you want to know who I was down there with?"

I take the cigarette from her and shrug. "Hughsie?"

I know Stella has seen him again. Met him in a pub in town. Let him kiss her. Touch her. She says.

"Wrong answer. Gone off him. Too old. Kept talking about Oasis and Blur. And he's got all these wrinkles around his eyes." She exaggerates a shudder.

I am relieved. I hated knowing what she was doing. It felt dirty, to be part of the secret.

"Come on, then."

"I don't know. Ed?" As if, I think.

"No. Lose two hundred pounds and forfeit a turn. Think blonder. Richer."

I hesitate. Because I don't want it to be him. But of course it is. "Blair."

"Ding-ding. Right answer."

"What about Emily?" I say.

"What about her?" Stella scoffs. "She doesn't own him, you know."

"Tell *her* that."

"Whatever." Stella dismisses me. "Anyway, he says we're invited to a party later. Matt's parentals are away, so it's an all-nighter."

"Really?" I am wondering why Ed hasn't said anything. Maybe he thinks I can't hack it. After last time. That I'm still a schoolkid who can't hold her liquor. Who doesn't fit into his life anymore. His world.

"Yeah, really. You coming? Or is your social calendar too packed?"

And I think about them. Ed, Emily, the Plastics. And I think, *I'll show them who I am. Who I can be.*

I laugh. "Well, I'd love to." I put on my best southern belle. "But I don't have a thing to wear."

"You must have." Stella sighs.

I lose the Blanche DuBois. "I don't. I've worn that black dress to death. . . . Can't I borrow something of yours?"

Stella sits up, her face lit with a eureka moment. "I have a better idea."

"No, Stella . . ." It is going to involve stealing, or something illegal, I know it. Neither of us has any money.

Stella looks at me as if she has discovered a cure for cancer. "Charlie."

"What?" I don't get it. I think she means coke, cocaine. But it's not. It's something else. Just as dangerous.

"Charlie. Your mum. Eighties poster girl. There must be tons of her stuff from photo shoots stashed away."

Then I know what is coming. "Yeah, but . . ."

"But nothing. Oh, God, I bet she has a Lagerfeld."

"Um. Maybe."

"What? You don't know?"

I don't. I was still a kid when they were packed away. Miniskirts down to my ankles and heels so big I would wade around the house, clopping like a country horse. But Dad didn't like seeing me in them. Reminding him of what he didn't have. Of what happened. So now they lie mothballing in the attic.

"Jude! You've got your very own Dixie's in the house and you're wearing a T-shirt that cost three pounds."

"I don't know, Stell." But I do. I want to see. Want to dress up again.

And she knows it.

"It's a waste of good fashion, otherwise. Come on. She'd want you to wear them. Pretty please . . ." She pouts.

I can't argue. She is already backing out of the door, and I follow her, like I always do.

I feel like I'm opening the Ark of the Covenant. Sitting in the dust of the attic floor. Not sure what angels or demons are going to fly out of the trunk and possess me. I pull aside the catches, rusting now, and slowly lift the lid, half expecting golden light to pour out, shining from the treasure within.

And it is treasure. Westwood. Dior. Galliano. The names wink at me, saying, *I told you so.* I touch a violet minidress. The smell of her wafts up, overpowering. Like someone packed her into a case and shut the lid on her. Preserving her for me to find now that I'm sweet sixteen.

"Oh . . . my . . . God!" Stella looks like she has won the lottery. She pulls out a boned strapless thing, tiny waist, miniskirt billowing out like a tutu. "Gaultier. It is so going to fit me." She holds it against herself and strikes a pose. "How do I look?"

I stare at Stella draped in iridescent blue silk and black lace, standing among the trunks and boxes and broken things of the attic. But all the time I am seeing her. Mum. Getting ready for a Christmas party. I must have been six or seven. Alfie not even inside her yet. She is coming down the stairs with a champagne glass in her hand, singing "The Stripper" as she high-kicks for me. Dad and I laugh and cheer, and he wolf-whistles as she blows him a kiss. I don't want her to have it. Stella, I mean. It's mine.

"I'm wearing it."

"Huh?"

"That's what I'm going to wear. That dress. The Gaultier."

Stella lets it fall, but still holds on to it, not relinquishing it without a fight. "But it's so me. And you haven't even looked at the rest yet."

"Please, Stell."

She throws it at me. "Whatever . . . jeez. But I'm having a Westwood."

"Fine," I reply. And it is. I don't care about the other dresses. Just this one.

* * *

I can hear Dad and Alfie playing Trivial Pursuit in the front room. Alfie knowing who was the first man on the moon and the third James Bond and the last king of Scotland. I am standing in the hall, wearing the Gaultier, cleavage out, lips red. The color of blood. Of sex.

I walk in.

And I wait for the Ark of the Covenant to open again and hell and damnation to rain down on me. Dad stares, trying to work it out. And then he gets it, and I see a flicker of recognition across his face. He can see her — that night — and he is mesmerized. Caught in the memory.

Alfie is delighted. "I can see your boobs."

"Shut up, Alfie." Because what he thinks doesn't matter. I don't want him spoiling this.

But Dad is lost, frozen in another place and time.

"So?" I say impatiently. Daring him to tell me to take it off.

"Where did you get it?" he says finally.

I know he is holding it back, like the little boy with his finger in the dam, and it could go at any minute. Could burst out of him. All the things he wants to scream, to shout. And this time I want to hear it, want to know what it is that stalks him at night. This ghost that won't leave him. Is it that I'm not her, and he wishes I were? Wishes she were here instead of me? Or is it that he's scared I am too like her. That I am her. I will him to say it. To tell me. Now, when he's not drunk. Now, when I am strong. Bold. Beautiful.

"The attic," I say, the words my sugar cube, my trail of pebbles, luring him into a trap. And it has worked. I watch as his mouth opens, wait for the words to come.

But Alfie speaks too quickly. "Dad, can I go in the attic? Can I?" His face is alive with thoughts of hidden treasures.

And the reverie is gone. The moment lost.

"Jude, put something on over that." Dad's voice is harsh, his face set.

"Told you," Alfie gloats, quietly triumphant.

I look up at the ceiling. Begging my fairy godmother to come down now. To wave her wand. But there's just cracked plaster and cobwebs.

I look down, back at him, waiting for an answer. "It's too hot for anything else," I snap.

He tries again. "I want you home by eleven."

But I'm on fire. I'm burning hot, burning bright. "Don't wait up."

I turn. Then I click-clack out of the room in the same heels that carried her down the stairs that Christmas. And I know each sound punctures him. Because it punctures me too.

Ed watches us walk down the path to Matt's. Every-one watches us. "Let them," Stella says. "We're bloody beautiful."

"Jude." Ed reaches out to grab my arm.

"That's her name. Don't wear it out," Stella shoots.

"I didn't think you'd be allowed to come, after last time. Didn't want you to get into trouble."

"Whatever," I say.

And Stella laughs as I pull her away. Looks at Ed over her shoulder and says, "Nobody puts Baby in a corner."

I have lost Stella. Last seen downing Pernod and Black—an homage to eighties tastelessness, apparently, to go with her dress. I am too hot. I need water or Coke or something. I open the fridge door and let the cool fluorescent air hit me. Breathe in the smell of salad cream and cold chicken.

Someone reaches in and grabs a bottle. Then shuts the door, plunging me back into the heavy heat, cutting off my air supply.

Blair. I look at him in the half-light. Blond streaks slicing into his preppy cut. Polo shirt and cutoffs. And he's looking right back. At the dress. At me underneath it. My heart beats faster. Fear, or desire. God, no.

"Emily's outside," I warn.

"I know."

He moves closer. I feel his breath on my face. "Don't you scrub up nicely?" He touches the end of his Bud on my breast. The condensation trickles down, staining the silk. I push him away.

"Get lost, Blair."

He smiles. "You're such a tease, Jude."

"As if."

He shrugs. "I'll get what I want in the end."

"What are you going to do?" I sneer. "Slip me a roofie?"

"Like I need to."

I roll my eyes. "In your dreams."

"But you are." He backs away, still smiling his alligator smile.

"You OK?"

It's Ed, giving me this weird look as I drain a bottle of Bud. I open the fridge and take another. As if this is normal. As if this is me. "Checking up on me, are you?"

He touches my arm. "No. I . . . I just want to see you."

I strike a pose. "So here I am. Seen enough?"

"God. What's wrong with you, Jude? You're like . . . I don't know . . . Jekyll and Hyde at the moment. I never know where I stand."

I know he's right. And I know why. Because with Stella there's no room for anyone else. No room for him. But I can't tell him that. So I just push him away. Like I did before.

"You can stand wherever you want."

Ed looks down, defeated. Almost. He raises his eyes. "Just don't do anything . . . stupid."

I laugh, holding his gaze. Then I turn and walk straight out into the bullring.

"Nice dress, Polmear." Emily holds up a bottle of Bacardi to toast me in sarcasm. Dawce laughs.

I swing around. "Yeah? Give my regards to Blair. Tell him I might just take him up on his offer."

I grab a glass off the table and half fill it with something. Anything. I down it. Ugh. Pernod. Like aniseed balls but worse. The alcohol pumps through me with the thudding beat of the music. The house smells sweet, heavy with dope.

"Wanna dance?" Someone grabs my hand.

And I don't care whose it is. I just let them take me. Take me somewhere. Anywhere.

19

I WAKE up in my bed, my legs wound around Stella's. She is asleep, mouth open, her breath stale with last night's smoke. Sickly smell of aniseed hanging over her. Still wearing the Westwood dress and cowboy boots. I am in my bra and knickers, the Gaultier crumpled in a heap on the floor. I can see a tear in the back. I look at the clock and groan. It reads 4:00 p.m. I can't remember getting home. God. Why do I do it? Still, at least I made it back. At least I'm not on Ed's floor again.

I need to pee. I untangle my legs and sit up. Dizziness sweeps over me. I lean forward, head in my hands. Stella turns over and pulls the covers tighter around herself.

I lower my feet to the floor, walk shakily to the

bathroom, sit down on the cool white of the toilet seat. The pee stings me. I realize my whole body hurts. There are bruises on my legs. Bruises I don't remember getting.

I flush the toilet and walk quickly back to my bedroom. Climb back into bed.

Stella lifts her head. "Oh. It's you."

"Who'd you think it was?"

"Dunno. No one." She lets her head drop and closes her eyes again.

I want to ask her about the bruises. If she knows. But she won't. She wasn't around.

"Where'd you go last night?" I ask.

"What do you mean?"

"You disappeared. Remember?"

She smiles. "Oh, yeah."

"So?"

"Do we have to do this now? I don't feel well." She pulls the cover over her head. Turns her back.

And then it's not me I'm worrying about anymore. It's her. What she's done.

"Stella." I feel panic rising up in me like stomach acid. Silence.

"Come on, Stell. What did you do?"

She rolls onto her back, pulls down the cover, and stares at the ceiling. "Well, put it this way. We got back at Emily Applegate."

And I never believed it when I read it in books. That it could really happen. But I swear, right then, my heart missed a beat. I force the words out. "What do you mean?"

"What do you think I mean?"

And I am there. See her touching him. See him push her dress up. Hear him beg. Please. Oh, God. Eyes closed. Her watching him the whole time. Smiling. Not even caring what it means. I feel sick.

"Blair? You let him . . . Why?"

"You know why."

So he found what he really wanted. Her. And even though I don't want him, something inside me is bruised now, hurt. Because he wanted her more.

"Where?" I say quietly.

"Matt's room."

"Where was Emily?"

"Passed out in the garden. She and Dawce were on pills."

I feel the sickness turn to fear. Anger. "At least tell me you used something."

"What's it to you?" Stella is groping around for her cigarettes now. Agitated.

I flinch. "Nothing." But it is so not nothing. I remember Blair at the fridge, touching me with the bottle. The way he looked. The way he spoke. Like he could have anyone. "He tried it on with me, you know."

"Yeah, right." She lights up.

"He did," I insist. "But I had the sense to tell him where to go."

145

She laughs as she blows out smoke. "You're just jealous. Because you're not me. Because you're a virgin. And you always will be. Unless you let Fat Ed do it out of sympathy—"

"Shut up," I say slowly.

But she doesn't listen. "Christ, Jude. You're so uptight, you couldn't even do your own audition. It's pathetic. You're nothing. And you have the bloody gall to criticize me."

I don't want to hear it, don't want to hear what I am. I snap. "Get out!" I yell. "Just get out!"

"Jesus, Jude. What's the matter?"

"I hate you. I hate you." I kick and thrash my arms to get her away from me.

Then Dad is in the room and he's shouting at me to calm down. I'm thinking, *Shit, Stella's still here,* my head thumping with the drink and the smoke. Dad snatches the cigarette and throws it out of the window. Then he's holding me down. Begging me to stop. And she leaves. Leaves me to him. I start to cry, great heaving sobs. And I cry until there are no tears left.

Dad stares at an invisible speck on the wall, like he can't even bear to look at me.

"What time did you come in last night?" he says to the speck.

"I don't know," I say. Truth.

"Four," he says. "Four in the morning, Jude."

"Why'd you ask if you knew?"

He shakes his head at the speck. "Aren't you even going to say sorry?"

"For what? Having a few drinks? Big deal," I sneer.

"It is a big deal, actually." He looks at me finally. I see disgust in his face. And something else. Fear. "It's not just the drinking, Jude."

"What, then?"

"Do you need me to spell it out for you?"

I shrug. "I guess so."

"The coming in late, the smoking."

"That wasn't me," I protest.

"Jude."

"It wasn't."

He looks at the speck again, his fists clenched. "I can't do this, Jude. I don't know who you are these days."

"I'm me . . . I'm still me. Christ. Just because I'm not Daddy's little girl anymore."

He shakes his head. Speaks quietly. "You never were."

I was hers. Always hers. It was Mum I went to when I fell over, or fell out with anybody. Mum who shared my secrets.

"Tell me what to do," he says. But I don't know who he's talking to now. Me or her.

"Nothing," I say eventually. "You do nothing."

"I want you to see someone. Talk to someone."

"A shrink? You've got to be kidding me. What's she going to say? 'Tell me about your childhood'? So I can just blame it all on my mother."

147

I stop, cover my mouth. Because I know I've gone too far.

I see it in his eyes. The built-up frustration. The fear. He lets it out. Hitting me across my cheek, his hand smacking against my jawbone. And then I'm crying again. Railing. Against him. Against my life. Against everything.

"When will you get it?" I yell. "I'm not her. I'm nothing like her. I bloody wish I were. But I'm not. I'm Jude . . . I'm Jude."

And he's crying too. Part of me just wants him to hold me tight. Like I've cut my knee or fallen off a swing. But we both know we're past that. Or we were never there at all. So I take the easy route and walk out the door. Exit heroine, stage right. No applause.

20

I GO where I always go. Up to the Point. Don't want to deal with last night's fallout, the casualties down in the dunes. Emily and the Plastics nursing bottles of Evian. Blair acting like nothing happened. God knows where Stella is. I don't want to see her.

I eat two bags of crisps and down a carton of OJ. Nicked from the shop. The juice is warm and the acid hurts my throat and stomach, a ball of pain reminding me of last night's excess. As if I need reminding.

I look out into the open water. Sun sparkling on the deep blue, waves studded with white flecks. Whitecaps trying to reach the shore. I love the sea. Its smell, the sting of salt spray, the sound. Blocking out everything. Bigger than anything we can make.

I remember the sound of London. The drone of cars and sirens and the heavy beat of reggae and hip-hop. The noise of people blocking out nature. No sea there to swallow it up. And the smell. Hot tar and takeaway food and sweat and exhaust fumes. A disgusting soup of human nature. But beautiful and beguiling too.

Then I remember Stella's words. "You're nothing. Nothing without me." And London, my life less ordinary, fades, and all I can see is the endless sea, stretching out, engulfing me, drowning me.

"Beautiful, isn't it?"

The voice is as familiar to me as Dad's or Alfie's. I don't need to turn around. But I do. Ed is standing behind me, hands shielding his eyes from the sun, curls blowing into his face in the warm air.

I look away again. "What is?"

"The sea."

"I wasn't thinking about that." I start poking a stick into the sandy soil, wondering why he's always there when I need him. "Did you know I was going to be here?" I say.

"I tried the house," he replies. "Your dad said you'd had a fight."

I feel my cheeks redden. Because I know why he told him. Reliable Ed. He'll sort me out. Persuade me to give up the drink and the cigarettes and the bad, bad company. Whoever it is.

He sits next to me. Touches my arm. I pull away.

"I told you I don't need checking up on."

"I'm not checking up on you, Jude." He stops, looking for the words. "I . . . I just wanted to see you. We used to hang out every day. Now you never call. And when I do see you, half the time you shout at me. Or ignore me. And I know I sound like a cheesy film or something, but, Jude, I don't know what else to say."

I shrug. I know it's true. But I don't know what to say to make it right again. For a second I think about "sorry." But it won't come out.

Ed keeps digging. "So, what was last night about? You and Blair?"

"Nothing happened."

"Whatever." He pauses. "You know he'll never dump Emily."

"Like I care. I told you, nothing happened. Whatever you saw—whoever you saw—it wasn't me. Jesus. As if. You know I wouldn't go near him. And like he'd come anywhere near me, anyway." Tears prick my eyes.

"Hey, Jude." He nudges me. "I'm sorry. I just thought—"

"Well, you thought wrong." I am crying now. Can't stop. Where do they all come from? The tears. I remember a fact that Alfie told me. How many liters of tears are cried in England every day. Something like a hundred thousand. I feel like they're all mine.

151

"Hey, hey. It's OK."

"No, it's not." My breath is labored. Gasping.

Ed reaches for my hand. I let him take it.

"Why didn't you tell me about the party?" I ask.

"I didn't see you," he says.

I shake my head. "You could have called. Come over. Or, what, you've forgotten my number? Where I live?"

He lets my hand drop. Pushes his hair back. Pulls at a thread on his T-shirt. I wait.

"OK, truth. I wanted to. But . . . sometimes you scare me, Jude."

"Sometimes I scare myself," I whisper.

He looks away. My stomach turns again. At what I've done to me. To him. Then I say it. That word. "Sorry. I'm sorry . . ." I start to shake as the sobbing starts up again. And then he's holding me, stroking my hair, like she used to. Calming me down.

The crying peters out and my breathing slows. But he doesn't stop. And I don't want him to. I can feel his breath hot on my neck. The hand pressed hard on my waist starting to move. Touching my back. Then everything goes slow and I know what's going to happen, seen it so many times in films. But never to me. Not until now. I move my head and look up. He's looking down at me. Into me. Like he's asking me if it's OK. If I want to. And I do. God, I do. Then he's kissing me, his lips soft, tugging at mine, his tongue sweet vanilla and salt, and I swear it's the best thing I have ever tasted. He pulls away and looks at me.

I am scared he's thinking he's made a mistake and is going to walk away. "What's wrong?" I am breathing hard.

"Do you . . . ? Are you . . . ?"

But I don't say anything. I pull him back to me and kiss him this time. Harder. My hands riding up under his T-shirt. Touching his chest. And I feel a surge of want. Feel him against me. He moans and pushes into me. I glance toward the village. There is no one at the Point but us. No one to stop us. I pull Ed's T-shirt up, over his head. And I look at this body I've grown up with, seen a thousand times. But never like this. I take his belt buckle in my fingers.

"Jude?"

He touches my face. Wants to know if I am OK. I kiss his hand and pull the belt undone. I want this.

Then he's pushing my skirt up. His fingers reaching for me. And part of me is scared. Because it's Ed. Because it's me. Because this is what Stella would do. Except it doesn't feel sleazy, like with her and Blair. Or Hughsie. It feels right. I'm not standing on the outside, looking in. I'm here. It's happening to me. There is no sound of the sea. No wind. Nothing. I am just inside my head. Reduced to a feeling.

"Have you got anything?"

Ed opens his eyes, nods. He reaches for his wallet, pulls out a foil-wrapped packet. I smile. Not caring that it might have been meant for someone else. Not caring that he might have done it before. Just glad it's there.

He looks at me. "Are you sure?"

"Yes." And I kiss him again.

And I think, *I love you. I love you.*

"I love you." Ed is holding me, our bodies entangled. He kisses my forehead and pushes my hair back so he can see me clearly. "I always have, Jude."

"I love you too." The words sound odd, spoken aloud. Words I've said to no one for so long.

"Now we really do sound like a film."

I laugh. He pulls me tight, and we stay like that until the evening air turns our skin to goose bumps, until we remember where we are, where I have to go. To face Dad. To mumble sorry, and wait for him to do the same.

I sit up, shivering. Pull my clothes on. I watch Ed, his back to me as he gets dressed, red marks where I have grasped him. On my back, too, where it has been pushed into stones on the ground under me. He turns and smiles, and I smile back, at the weirdness, and the rightness, of it all.

He walks me home. We don't say anything. Don't need to. Outside the shop he pulls me to him and kisses me. I feel myself disappearing again. The streetlights, the pub, all gone. But I know we can't. Not here. And not inside either. Not tonight. I drop my head and drink in the smell of him. He kisses my hair.

Then he's walking away up the hill, his eyes still on me. "See you tomorrow, yeah?"

I smile. "Not if I see you first."

He grins. And is gone.

Dad is slumped at the table. There's no bottle this time, but I smell it on him. The bittersweet tang of whiskey. But I have my secret too. I am drunk on Ed. On the beauty of him. Of us.

He stands, scraping the chair across the floor. "Jude, I'm so sorry."

"Me too." It's a whisper, my eyes on the floor.

"I don't know why I . . ." He trails off.

Then this feeling fills the silence. This possibility. That he will open his arms and reach out to me.

I look up, hopeful. But his arms hang by his sides. Closed.

It's gone. And I want to get away from him now. Back to my room. To my secret.

I force a smile. "'Night, Dad."

"'Night."

I lie on my bed. The curtains are still open, letting in the moon and stars, dappling my skin.

Alfie crawls in and burrows under the covers next to me.

"Where did you go?" he asks.

"Just out, Alfie."

"With Stella?" he asks.

I start. "No." Then softer, "We had a fight."

"Like with Dad?"

"Kind of."

"Do you want her to come back?"

In my head, I look out across the village. See the moon bounce off the slate of his roof. Imagine Ed lying there, his body still alive with me. And in that moment I know who I want. And who I want to be. And neither one is her. "No." I smile. "Not anymore."

But Stella has other ideas.

21

OF COURSE she comes back. She made a promise.

Ed has just left, gone to pick his brother up from the station. I am lying on my bed, my body still buzzing with the feel of him. I can't believe there was a time when we weren't like this, when we were nothing but friends. Not even that sometimes. Can't believe he's going away soon. It's been weeks and there's still no letter from the Lab. But I don't think about it when he's here. Don't think about anything. Because he makes me happy. I make me happy.

I hear someone on the stairs. *Alfie,* I think, wanting to go to the beach. Or to tell me that tomatoes are actually a fruit. But when I open the door, she's standing there in the Westwood dress, ripped now, Converse low-rises on her feet, dog tags around her neck. In case she gets lost. How Stella.

I don't know what to say. What I want to say.

"So, can I come in?" She tilts her head to one side. "If you're nice, I'll let you buy me a Slushie."

"What's that supposed to mean?"

"Nothing. Just, you know."

"No. I don't."

She walks past me and sits on the bed.

"Suits you."

I shut the door.

"What does?"

"Sex." She relishes the word.

"How can sex suit someone?"

"I don't know." She tuts. "It just does. You look better. Less Pollyanna."

"Gee, thanks." I throw her my best fake smile.

"Don't mention it." She picks up a CD. Throws it down. "So. You and Ed?"

I don't say anything. Not sure if I want to tell her. Knowing she'll want details. Things that are just ours. But she knows anyway.

"I'm pleased," she announces. "Seriously. So much better than Blair."

"Not hard," I say.

"God, get over it, Jude."

"I am. Anyway, not my problem."

Stella shrugs. "I would rather have thirty minutes of wonderful than a lifetime of nothing special."

I start. Something Mum used to say. "Where did you hear that?"

"I don't know. A film or something. Anyway, it's deep. And totally true." She grabs my cigarettes off the desk and takes one. Lights it up. Then throws the lighter and packet over to me. Ed wants me to stop. I know I should. Don't know why I ever started.

"So." She leans back. "Miss me, then?"

I laugh. Can't believe she's asking. "Jesus. You've got some nerve."

"Yeah. Well . . . I bet you did."

You're wrong, I think. *I didn't. Not once did I miss you. Not once did I wish you were here, instead of Ed. Because I don't need you anymore. I'm grown up. I can do it all by myself.*

Can't I?

"Why do you do it, Stella?" I say at last.

"Do what?"

I shake my head. "Mess up, then disappear."

"I didn't mess up," she says. "Or disappear. Just gave you some space. Looks like you made good use of it."

She lies back on the bed. "Is he good?"

"Stella—" I protest.

"Come on. I want to know. Is it Harlequin Romance? Some little bubble of teen magazine bliss?"

And my head is full of him again. His lips on mine.

Teasing. Pulling. His hands on my back. His eyes watching me. His words, his laughter, his love. The clumsiness and beauty of it all. I realize I'm smiling. And I want to tell someone how it feels.

"It's not like that." It's not like anything. Not like any film, or book, or *Cosmopolitan* article. It's everything and nothing I imagined.

"He's told you he loves you, hasn't he?"

I nod.

"What about you?"

"It's . . . you know." I want to explain what it feels like. The newness. And the safety of it. The peace. "It's . . . nice."

Stella scoffs. "Nice is for cups of tea or biscuits. It's not nice."

"OK. Amazing. It's bloody amazing. Happy now?"

"Not as happy as you, evidently."

"Ha, ha."

I look out the window and watch Mrs. Penleaze trudge up the hill, pulling a tartan shopping trolley behind her. I remember that day in the shop. Me and Stella laughing at her. Her daring me. And I feel a prick of shame. When I look back, Stella is in front of the mirror, fiddling with her hair. Putting it up and down in my cherry hair bobbles.

"Where did you go, then?" I ask.

"Nowhere." She pulls the hair elastic. It breaks. "Shit. Sorry." But she isn't. Just takes another and starts again.

I watch her watching herself. She pouts. Then picks

up a lip gloss. Squeezes out the fake watermelon goo and rolls it over her lips. "So, has Emily freaked about me and Blair?"

"No. She doesn't know. Well, I don't think she does. She's still with him." I saw them at Matt's. She was draped around him in the garden, Blair slapping Ed on the back, saying, "Nice one." Then some blah about double-dating, like we're in an episode of *Friends*. Then shooting me a look I don't understand. Worried, maybe, that I've told Ed about him and Stella. That I'll tell Emily. As if.

"Yeah, well. Her finding out isn't the point, anyway. It's us knowing that she's nothing. Not to Blair. Not to us." Stella looks at my reflection in the mirror. "OK. Million-dollar question. If you could be one person for a day, who would it be?"

"I don't know . . . the queen?" I don't mean it. But I don't feel like playing.

"Yawn. Cliché."

"Why? It'd be good," I lie.

"What, so you could give yourself thousands of pounds and abolish exams and things?"

"What's wrong with that?"

"Nothing. If you're eight years old."

"OK." I sigh. Grab another name. Anyone. "Mrs. Applegate, then. I'd get my stomach stapled and send Emily to the town high school."

"Better." Stella contemplates herself. "Know who I'd be?"

I think. Bound to be someone famous. Or dead. Or both. "I don't know. Greta Garbo?"

She shakes her head.

"Jackie Onassis?"

She rolls another layer of lip gloss on. "Not . . . even . . . close."

"Who, then?"

She blows her reflection a kiss, then smiles at mine. "You."

"What?" Not sure if she's joking. Not sure if I heard her right.

"I'd be you."

I look at myself. My roots growing out. Lipstick kissed off. My eyes, tired from late nights. I was a pale imitation of the original next to me, a cheap copy, a knockoff. But now I'm fading back into the old Jude underneath. The Jude I know I want to be now. But I don't understand why she does too.

She laughs. "You can't even see it, can you?"

And I should be happy that she wants to be me. That I'm somebody worth being. But instead I go cold. Because for a second there's something weird in the way she's looking at me. She was supposed to be my fairy god-mother. But what if she was the wicked witch all along? "I don't—"

"Doesn't matter," she says suddenly. "Forget it."

"Stella—"

She pauses. "OK. So I could . . . I don't know. Order American *Vogue*. Nick all the cigarettes from downstairs. Get myself a year's supply of stamps."

But she's lying. That look stays in my head. And it scares me.

22

THE LETTER arrives two days later. Ed and I are on my bed listening to a CD of some band he reckons is the Next Big Thing. Not doing anything else. Just lying next to each other. Like we always did. He's been over almost every day. Dad must know something is going on, suspect at least. But he hasn't flipped out. I think he's happy. Sees Ed as some sort of protector.

Alfie must have picked the envelope up. I hear him shrieking and thundering up the stairs. Dad telling him to calm down, not to run. But he bursts in anyway, eyes wide, talking so fast that I can't hear what he's saying.

"Hey." Ed turns down the music and moves his legs so my brother can climb on the bed with us.

Alfie pushes the envelope into my hand and I see the two short words printed in the corner. The Lab. Advertising its significance. Shouting it. Suddenly I feel dizzy, overwhelmed. My future on a piece of paper. In my hands. It seems wrong. These thin, weightless sheets for something so heavy.

"Open it, Jude," Alfie urges.

I'm still staring at the envelope. "I —" But I hear a noise and look up. Dad is in the doorway. Quieter than Alfie, but feeling the same. Hope, and fear. Just better at hiding it.

"I tried to stop him," he explains. "Thought you might want to do it in private, you know."

"It's OK."

"Would you like us to leave?"

I nod. I've never been one for audiences. Not in real life, anyway. On a stage it's different. You're someone else. But here, now, when I'm just me, I want to be alone.

"Come on, son."

"But, Dad —"

"But nothing. You can help me do the papers."

"Fine." He slips off the bed.

"You can come down to the beach with us later, mate." Ed grins. "Borrow the board, if you want."

"Can I?" Alfie is bursting again, looking at me for approval.

"Sure." I nod.

Alfie grins. "Dad says I can have your room if you get in."

I try to smile. But it's not funny. Not really. Because

what if I don't? What if I'm still here in three weeks, three months, three years? My hands shake. I push them into my lap to hide it.

"Downstairs. Now." Dad steers Alfie to the door and watches him clatter out. He is still for a second, trying to find the words. The courage.

"Good luck," he says finally. And I know he wants to mean it, at least.

"Thanks."

He closes the door. Then it's just me and Ed. And the letter.

"Do you want me to go too?" Ed touches my face. Moves my hair back. I press my cheek against his hand.

"No." I need him here, to hold me up. Or just to hold me.

I drop my head and look at the envelope, my hands still shaking, the knuckles white from gripping it.

"Jude, if you don't . . . If . . ."

He can't say it. If I don't get in.

"What I mean is, whatever happens, you know it won't change us."

I look at him. His dark eyes, the irises circled in black. His hair, longer now, touching his shoulders. Growing it for college, before the adult world makes him cut it off and wear a suit and tie. His lips soft, vanilla sweet. I touch them. He kisses my finger. And I close my eyes. Want that second to last forever. That image of him, the feel of him. The peace, and safety.

But I know I have to face things. I open my eyes.

"OK. Here goes nothing." I turn the envelope over in my hand. Slide my finger, still wet from the kiss, under the flap, and tear.

The letter is two pages, stapled. White vellum.

I read.

"Well? Come on, Jude, I'm dying here."

I hand him the letter. He scans the first line. All he needs. *I am delighted to offer you . . .* "Oh, my God, that's brilliant."

"Yeah," I say. And for a moment I believe it. I am elated, high on it, on the reality of it, of me leaving. But then I remember. It wasn't me who read the lines. Or sang pitch-perfect. It wasn't me who won the place. It was Stella.

I feel my heart beating and my stomach fill with butterflies, battering against the walls, trying to escape. I feel sick. Really sick. My mouth fills with saliva.

"Are you OK, Jude?" Ed asks. "You've gone white."

I don't answer. Can't open my mouth. Climb over him, run to the bathroom, and throw up.

Maybe I should call them, tell them there's been a mistake. I don't have to go. *I can stay here,* I think. *I'll be fine.*

But I won't. I want to go. I need to go.

Ed knocks on the door.

I look in the mirror. I am pale. Like a ghost of me.

"Jude?"

"Coming." I try to sound normal. Hide the fear in my voice.

I open the door.

"Eeuw. Must be the shock." Ed grins. "Lucky you didn't look like that when you auditioned. Check it out. You rock."

He hands me the second page of the letter. And there it is. My name. Address. Height. Singing range. Blah I must have filled out for the application. And at the top, a photo of me. Not the one I sent in, because this Jude has bleached hair, makeup. This photo was taken that day. My head spins. "Where did they get that?"

"What do you mean?" Ed looks confused. "They took it at the Lab, didn't they? One of those digital things? Like at the sports center."

I think back. Joan Crawford tapping a red fingernail on the keyboard. Staring at me and Stella. Asking my name. I don't remember a photo. *But, then, I was drunk,* I think. "I guess."

"You look hot."

"Thanks." But I'm not listening. I'm thinking, *If the photo is of me, then that's who they're expecting to show up, isn't it?*

"So, you want to tell your dad?"

"Uh . . . sure."

"I'll take Alfie down to the beach, then."

"Thanks."

"I'm so proud of you." He kisses my head. "Your dad

will be fine. Honest. And even if he isn't, he'll pretend to be."

I smile. "I know."

But as we walk downstairs, it's not Dad I'm worrying about. It's Stella. And what she'll say. And do.

Alfie jumps up and down on the sofa. Dad acts pleased. Like Ed said he would. Saying the words he knows he should.

"Well done, love. You deserve it."

"Thanks."

Then I think he's going to say it. But he stops. And I say it in my head for him, *Your mum would be proud.* And she would be. But, then, I think, *If she were here, would I want to leave?*

"We should call Gran."

I nod. I haven't told him yet that there's a spare room available in Ed's house. A four-bedroom in Battersea. Sharing with one of his brothers and some girl he knows — a third year at St. Martin's. The house is run-down, Ed says. No central heating. But no Gran, either, or being home by six, or endless questions, or watching her play bridge and get quietly drunk on Madeira.

"Later." I need to go out.

"When you get back, then. You'll want to tell your friends first." It's not a question, thank God. Because there's only one person I have to tell. I push the letter into my pocket and go to find her.

She's sitting on the wall outside the launderette, eating gummy cola bottles and jelly babies.

"Want one?"

"Thanks." I take a cola bottle. Feel the fizzy coating sting my tongue.

"So, what's new, pussycat?"

I pause, not sure whether to just blurt it out or to lead up to it. Not even sure why I'm worrying. I don't get the chance to decide.

"Oh . . . my . . . God. You got the letter, didn't you? Shit. Did you get in? I bet you did."

"Yeah."

"I told you I was good."

"I know."

She sees what I'm thinking. "You would have done it anyway, without me. If you hadn't been so strung out."

"Maybe."

"Not maybe. You would. Anyway, it doesn't matter now." She bites the head off a jelly baby.

"Do you remember this?" I hand her the sheet with the photo.

Stella looks at it, still chewing. "That's brilliant, huh?"

"When did they take it, though?"

"I don't know." She shrugs.

"But it can't have been at the audition," I say, "because I never went in."

"Must have been in reception."

"But when?"

"God, Jude." Stella swallows the sweet. "Who cares? You're in. They're expecting someone who looks exactly like you. What's not to like?"

"Nothing. Just . . . It feels weird."

"Get over it. You're going to Hollywood, baby!" She throws her arms open.

I sit down next to her. Smile. Trying it out.

Stella takes a cola bottle and stuffs it in her mouth, her legs dangling against the wall, kicking out. "OK. So do you think your gran's going to mind me staying there too? I mean, just for a while until we get somewhere. Oh, God. This is so cool. Unless we move back to Notting Hill. Then you can just stay with me. And Piers. Oh, you're going to love Piers. He will so fancy you—"

"Stell . . ."

"What? Oh, and you can meet Luella. She's that girl, the one I was telling you about. You know, she once—"

"Stella."

"What? Oh. OK. I get it. Tom won't approve. Well, we'll just let him down gently. Start off at Gran's and then, I don't know, say someone in your year has a room or something. Make out like it's really cheap, closer to the Lab."

"It's not that."

"What, then? Oh, wait. Don't tell me. Ed."

I don't say anything.

"You're not living with him? There is no way Tom will go for that."

"I'm sixteen."

"OK. Gran, then. Your sugar granny. She's paying, isn't she? Do you think she's going to let you shack up with someone who's screwing her darling granddaughter? Dream on."

"They like Ed."

"Of course they do. Now. Because he's 'nice.' But as soon as they find out he's had his hands down your hipsters, alarm bells are going to ring, believe me."

"Maybe." I cringe at the thought of them seeing me like that.

"Honest, Jude. It is never . . . going . . . to happen."

I say nothing. Because there's no point. Not now. I'll wait. Tell her before I go. Just leave her here. Or we can meet up in Portobello or something. Like Kate Moss and Sadie Frost. Trawling the stalls for vintage. But, somehow, I know that's not what she's planning.

"So, party tonight?"

"Sure." And I smile. So she can see it's fine. That she's right.

But as she smiles back, I can see that she knows. Knows what I'm planning. That I don't want her anymore. Not just because of Ed. But because I want me. I want to be me. And I'm scared, because I know she'll find a way to stop it. She won't let me win. And I feel lost again. Small. Because I've started something I can't finish.

23

I AM leaning over the sink. Retching again. Seem to spend half my life throwing up. But this isn't cheap vodka or stolen Pernod. It is something else. Fear. Realization.

I don't know when I clicked about Stella and Ed. Just a look between them, that's all. A second. That night in the pub. We're all sitting, talking. Matt's telling everyone about this festival he's going to in Wales. I'm nodding, smiling. But all I can hear is Stella. She's talking to Ed, quietly. Telling him how amazing he is. That I'm lucky. And I see him smile. Laugh quickly at her cockiness. And then I see it. Under the table. Her hand on his thigh. Then moving up. He pauses, pushes it away. But that pause. And what he says. "Not here." I look away, hoping that I'm wrong, that I missed something. A joke perhaps. So I say nothing that night. Because anyone can slip like that. And Stella—I mean, who wouldn't want her to want them? Even Ed, who always held her in contempt. Part of him must think she's got something. Because it's not a maybe. She just has.

Then yesterday. I'm sitting on the wall outside the shop. Ed skates down the hill to say he's going to London today. Taking some stuff up to his brother's in the Land Rover. Asks if I want to come.

"Sure," I say.

Then Stella does her appearing trick. "Me too," she says. "I call shotgun."

Ed looks at me. I shrug.

"You'll have to navigate," he says.

"I can do more than that." She's got a finger in her mouth.

And he's laughing. But there's something else. Desire.

And then I knew something had happened between them. Maybe not even this week. Maybe a while ago. I replay the images in my head. Her going into his room, in the dark. All he can see is blond hair. Smell of Chanel. And I bet she's better than me. Knows what to do. Done it before. And then he sees who it is. Hates himself for not knowing. But wants her anyway. His eyes closed, hands on her, pushing her down. And she's watching him. Not even enjoying it, just what it means. That she's won.

Or maybe they haven't even done it. Maybe they've just kissed. I don't know. Don't want to know. Whatever, it's the same in the end. Means the same thing. That he wants her more than he wants me. And that she wants him. Because he's the one thing I've got that she doesn't. And she thinks he's the one thing keeping us apart, me and her. Because I wouldn't be able to do it by myself. Poor little Jude. Jude the Obscure.

I retch again, but there's nothing left but bile. I flush the toilet. Go back to my room. Put on some music. And wait.

Ed comes around in his Land Rover, ready to leave. He wants to get there before rush hour and the Land Rover only does sixty at a push. I can hear him talking to Dad downstairs. About his plans. And the house. We still haven't told him. No need now, I think.

I hear the familiar footsteps on the stairs. Then he's in my room. Wearing a faded T-shirt and jeans. Classic Adidas he bought off eBay, the same day I got my fake fur coat. For London winters. Like Anita Pallenberg, he said. Like Stella, I thought. Like my mum. Before she wanted to ban the fur trade and started sticking chewing gum on mink coats at Harrods.

"Ready?" Ed looks around. "Where's your bag?"

I haven't packed. I'm not going. Can't go. Not now.

"What's up?" He sits down. Touches my leg.

"Don't." I pull it away.

"Jude? What's going on?"

I look at the floor, willing it to swallow me. So I don't have to do this.

It doesn't oblige, so I'm forced to speak, before he touches me again.

"Why are you here?"

His forehead creases, not understanding. "What?"

"You don't have to pretend, you know."

"Jude, I have no idea what you're talking about."

He is lying.

"I saw you," I say, my insides churning with the memory. "The way you looked at her."

"Who?"

I laugh. Hollow. Bitter. "You know who."

But he won't say it. Won't admit it. "Look, I don't know what this is about. Or who this is about." His voice is patient. But I hear patronizing. "I don't care about anyone else. It's you I want. You, Jude."

"I don't believe you. I saw you," I repeat. I can feel my face wet with tears now.

"What? I've got no idea what you're talking about." Patience gone, he is angry now. "I can't believe I'm defending myself. What is wrong with you, Jude? I thought all this . . . self-esteem stuff, or whatever it is, was sorted out."

"It's not about self-esteem, is it?" I cry. "It's about you."

"Jude, just tell me what's wrong. Tell me and I can help."

I say nothing. Just wipe my face, defiant. But the tears keep on coming.

"I can't do this." He looks out the window. Away from me shaking on the bed, staring at the floor.

He turns back. "Jude, I have to leave. Are you coming?"

I shake my head.

"Fine."

Silence. I wait for him to go.

But he doesn't.

"I love you, Jude. No one else. Never have."

I say nothing.

"I'll be back tomorrow night. I'll come around."

I shrug. "Don't bother."

"Have it your way." Then, softer, "Call me, then. Please." He pauses. "You have to sort this out. And I can help you if you want. But you have to trust me."

I'm still looking at the floor. Waiting. Willing him to go.

He does. The back door slams shut and the Land Rover chokes into life, revs, his foot pushing hard on the accelerator. Then it trails off, out of the village. Heading to London.

Dad shouts up the stairs. "Jude, you all right?"

I wipe my face again. Shout back, making sure my voice doesn't crack. "Yeah."

"Thought you were going to London."

"Not this time." I smile through the tears. Because if I sound happy, he'll go.

"OK. Well, I've got to go out. Mrs. Hickman is here. I'll be back by midday."

I say nothing. Can't speak.

"Bye, Dad," he says to himself. I hear him smiling. Like he's told the funniest joke in the world.

The door shuts and I'm alone. The sobs rack through me again, because however much I want to trust Ed, I know I can't. Because I know what she's like. She never gives up. She always gets what she wants. There's nothing he can do.

Not that she really wants him. She's never loved him. She's always said he was a loser. Someone who followed. Who would never do anything to astound the world. That he was a small-town boy. That even if he went to London, he'd never stay. He'd always end up in Churchtown. Like Dad. Give up on the life he thought he wanted and settle for this one.

She said that I was different. That I would leave my life and never come back. That I would shimmer and glitter and be loved. And I smiled. Because I wanted to shine alongside her. Because I thought she was helping me. But she was just helping herself.

I cry. Harder than I have ever cried before. Because that life is in reach, the life I wanted. Glittering. But to get it, I have to lose them both. Ed and Stella. My best friends. The emptiness is overwhelming. A gaping hole in me. But then something creeps into the gap. Anger at what she's done and what I've let her do to me. All that "There's no me without you" stuff.

My fingers ache. And I realize they are clenched tight. My stomach, too. I need to find her. To tell her to stop. To end it. I don't want to be us anymore. I just want to be me.

24

I KNOW she hasn't gone with him. Doesn't need to now that she's gotten what she wanted. To break us up. So she can keep me to herself. I can feel her, feel that she's nearby. Like those TV psychics who can see ghosts. I can see Stella.

She's not in the village. Just tourists buying bread and newspapers, making sure they haven't missed anything in the outside world, the real world. *I'm coming with you,* I think. I'm getting closer. Warmer. If I can just do this one last thing. I leave the cool granite shade behind me and head for the dunes.

* * *

The beach is packed. High season, every bit of sand deco-rated with beach towels and tents. The sea full of surf-ers, bodyboarders, and squealing children, shocked by the Atlantic cold and the undertow. I walk along the water's edge. Easier here where the sand's wetter, harder. In the sand-sinking dunes, Duchy girls are stretched out in SPF 8, ignoring every cancer warning. Too young and too vain to take it seriously. I look for Emily and the Plastics. For Blair. But it's too early. They'll be sleeping off whatever excesses they enjoyed last night.

I reach the rocks at the foot of the Point. No one on the ledges now. Too many lifeguards to shout warnings. Dog walkers to report them, note down their license plates.

Only one more place to try. Her home. My old one. I turn on to the cliff path and start the long walk to the farm.

It smells different. That's the first thing I notice. Not the power-washed stone, or the new tarmac of the car park, once our yard, with its chalked hopscotch and tricycles, a playground for me and the chickens. Not even the cur-tains in the windows of the old calving barn; people walk-ing, sleeping, eating in a room that has seen pints of blood and shit over its floor, heard the bellows of birth, the first breath of the newborn, and the last of the runts. No, what hits me first is that the sweet, warm smell of cows, of life and death, has been built over, scrubbed away, taking gen-erations of Polmears with it.

There are five cottages now: the farmhouse in the middle and the others squeezed into the barns and out-houses around the yard. Seaview is on the end, part of the milking shed. Stella is right: there's no way you can see the sea from there. Not unless you stand on the roof. Which we did, of course, before Dad screamed at us to get down and I swung around to see him and slipped any-way. Scraping my arms and legs on the tiles. But not fall-ing. Because Stella held on to my arm. Dad said it was the gutter that did it, jamming my foot just in time. But I knew it was her.

There's no car in the parking space. I look through the window and see rough burlap carpets, a white Shaker table and chairs, checkered cushions. Some London designer's idea of beach-hut chic. Not like the homes in the village, all swirly carpets, brass fittings, and porcelain dairymaids on the mantelpiece.

I strain to see the detritus of life with Stella. Bottles of nail varnish, tops left off. Coke cans. Half-smoked ciga-rettes. But all I can see are empty coffee cups. A *Times*. And books. A John Grisham on the table, dog-eared half-way through. A Marian Keyes, glittery blue with pink lettering. So not Stella. No *On the Road* or *Prozac Nation*. No Shelley or Keats. I don't bother to knock. I've seen enough to know that no one is home.

I'll come again, I think. Try later. Maybe they're in town. Her dad's exhibition must have started by now. So I'm walking away, past the wall, rough wood sanded now, the chalk lines that measured my upside-down handstand height painted over. And I think, *One last time*. No one around to see me now. I step forward, hands in front of me and push down.

That's when she shows up. Walks into my sight line. Enter villainess, stage right, eating an ice-cream bar.

"Nice knickers. Bet Ed loves them."

I drop down and turn to face her.

She picks off a piece of chocolate, licks vanilla ice cream off her fingers. "Want a bite?"

I wanted to hear her say it. Admit it. Needed to ask her. When. Why. But now that I'm here, the words won't come out.

I shake my head.

"Suit yourself." She shrugs. "Thought you were going to London."

"Thought *you* were," I counter.

Stella ignores me. "You and Ed fallen out? Did he pull your pigtails when you were playing chase-and-kiss?"

"We're not kids."

"Yeah, right." She picks off another piece of chocolate. Puts it in her mouth, closing her lips over her fingers.

I think of her touching him. Doing the things I have done. And things I haven't. Blood rushes to my head and I lurch against the wall.

Stella watches me with detached interest. "You need to stay off the drink."

"You bitch." The words are quiet. Deliberate.

"Pardon?"

"You heard me."

Stella laughs. "Let me get this straight. Is this about me? Or Ed? Because, believe me, I didn't have to try too hard."

I put my hand out and clutch at the wall to stop myself from falling. Any hope that she would convince me somehow that I was wrong, that I was overreacting, was now gone.

"But why?" The words are barely audible. "You know how I feel about him."

"You know why. I did it for you. Because if it weren't me, it would have been some first-year undergrad. Then you'd have been stuck in London without either of us. Better to find out now." She closes her mouth around the end of the vanilla. Sucks hard.

"You are unbelievable," I manage to spit out.

"That's why you love me." She pouts.

I look at her, standing there in her secondhand sundress and Ray-Bans, wedge heels on her feet. And I think, *I did love you, at first. When you curled your finger and beckoned me out of the shell I had built around myself. When you made me stronger, brighter than I ever thought I could be. But now you've made me into this person, into this version of you, and you want to destroy it. Or keep it for yourself. So I don't love you. Not anymore.*

"I can't do this," I say out loud.

"What?" Stella frowns.

I drop my head, finding the strength, breathing the warm air in lungfuls. My heart pounding. Because this will be it. This will be the end of it all.

I look up. "Us," I say.

She pauses, weighing the word up, eyes never moving from mine. Then she smiles. But it's not happy. It's not kind. It's the smile of someone who knows they have already won. "But there is no me without you," she says.

"Stella, I'm being serious."

"So am I."

I lose it. "I don't need you anymore. Get it?"

She takes the ice cream out of her mouth. Looks at me hard. "God, you're an ungrateful little cow."

"Ungrateful?" The word hits me like a sucker punch. "What have you done for me? Except dye my hair and steal my boyfriend."

"Yeah? Before me you were nobody. Jude the Obscure. You looked like a loser. And acted like one. Christ, you were still doing handstands and playing board games with your little brother on Saturday nights." She drops the ice cream on the ground.

I feel my fists clench and my eyes sting with salt water and truth. "So why'd you pick me, then? Some kind of charity project?"

"Something like that." She pulls a pack of cigarettes from under her bra strap. Lights one. The smell of her lighter turns my stomach.

"Yeah? Well, I didn't need it."

Stella blows a smoke ring. Watches it expand and disappear against the blue sky. Snaps the lighter shut and looks at me again. For the first time I see pity in her eyes. Disgust.

"I gave you an identity," she says.

"Yeah, whose? You turned me into someone else."

She shakes her head. "I turned you into who you wanted to be."

"What, you?"

"Yeah. And don't pretend you didn't love it." Her eyes narrow. "Why do you think Ed wanted you all of a sudden?"

"That's not true."

"Whatever." She folds her arms.

Tears run down my face. I wipe them away. "I don't know who I am anymore, Stella. I don't even know who you are. I mean, who are you? You disappear. You're not living in Seaview — unless you've turned into some thirty-something chick-lit fan."

Stella is silent, never one to miss a chance to milk a dramatic pause. Then she drops the cigarette, watches it smolder on the burned, yellowed grass. "You know who I am." She pauses. Then she looks me straight in the eyes. "I'm you, Jude."

"What?" I stare at her, not understanding.

"I'm you," Stella repeats slowly. "We're the same person. See?"

She takes my hand and puts it on her face. I can feel

her, but it's not like when I touch Ed or he touches me. It's as if I'm touching myself. I can feel the hand and the cheek. I am entranced. Lost in the surreality. Then she smiles. The smile is mine.

I snatch my hand away. My chest constricts and I struggle to speak. "You're lying."

"Really? So it wasn't you who took money out of the till to pay for that dress?"

I shake my head. This is a mass-market paperback plot line. Some big-money Hollywood thriller. This isn't real. It isn't happening.

"No? What about the audition, then? That photo. It was taken inside the audition room, Jude. Inside it. Because it wasn't someone else in there. It was you."

"But . . . you're here. Standing in front of me. I'm talking to you."

"Everyone talks to themselves. You get an answer back as well. Double the fun."

"No." I shake my head.

"Yes." Stella grabs my hand again. Holds it down on her cheek. On my cheek. "I am you. I look how you want to look. I talk how you want to talk. All the ways you wish you could be, that's me."

I recognize that line. And I feel nausea rise again. Because I realize what she's done. What I've done. And my head is full of images. Stella at the beach that first day back. Stella in my bedroom. Stella on the field at school, fiddling with her bra in front of Hughsie. Oh, God, Hughsie. I hold the wall. It wasn't Stella at the beach, kissing him, putting his hand on her. It was me. And the guy on the train. In the bathroom. And that night, Matt's party . . .

I turn to her. "Blair?"

Stella nods.

And I am back there. In Matt's room. Lying on the bed. I feel him again. Pushing inside me. And I remember the dull ache. The sting. The blood the next day. And I can't stop it then. I throw up, yellow spattering the wall. But it's not fear. Not vodka, or low blood sugar or shock or any other excuse I've passed off for the last week. I'm pregnant. And it's not Ed's. We've been too careful. It's Blair's.

She knows what I'm thinking. Of course she does. She is me. She's thinking it too.

"I did it for you, Jude. Because of Emily. I couldn't let her treat you like that. We couldn't . . . ."

I crouch down, one hand on my belly, trying to feel it inside me. This alien. I feel dirty. How could she? How could I? How could I do this to me, to Ed?

"You're only a few weeks in. You can have an abortion." She crouches down next to me. Puts her hand on my arm. "We'll be fine."

"We?"

"Yeah. I'll come with you. Hold your hand."

"No." I throw her arm off. She staggers backward. "Don't you get it? You have to go now. This has to stop."

"Just like that?"

"Yes." I nod.

Stella laughs. "But I can't."

"You can. Go . . . please," I beg. "Leave me alone."

"I'm not real, though, am I? You made me. I can't just walk away."

I shut my eyes. If she's just in my head, I can make her disappear. Can't I?

I open my eyes. She's still there, watching me crouched in my own vomit. She smiles. Holds out her hand to pull me up. My fairy godmother. "I'm everything you want to be. You said it yourself."

I look at her hand. Candy-pink nail varnish. Costume rings, my mum's, on the fingers. My hand. But this time I don't take it. I push myself up. And walk past her, back along the path. Home. And not once do I look back.

25

IT'S TWO in the morning. I'm lying in bed. Alone. Well, almost. Me and the thing inside me. I can't sleep. Not with it there. Part of me. And of him. I cringe as I see his face. At the fridge, his eyes following the trickle of water as it ran down my chest. Then again as he stared at me with Ed. Just days after I'd slept with him. I hear Blair saying my name. Not Stella. Jude.

I know now it was me and that Stella is just someone I've created, conjured up. My Frankenstein's monster. I go back over conversation after conversation, taking Stella out of the picture, making her words come out of my mouth. And she's right. It's me asking Emily what's her damage. Telling her she's got a fat girl's name. Lines from films. Ones I watched with Mum when she was too tired to take me to the beach. To school. That's where they all come from, Stella's put-downs. Mum's old videos. *Heathers, The Breakfast Club, Pretty in Pink.* American high-school stuff. The kind Dad hated. Because the teenagers were smart-mouthed.

Me telling Ed he's a lucky guy, touching him under the table. Him blushing, saying, "Not now." To me. Not to her. I feel relief for a brief second. That he didn't betray me. Then the horror seeps back in.

It all works. She was never there. It's like I've solved a Rubik's Cube. Or a Chinese puzzle from a Christmas cracker. Something has clicked into place, and now that it's there, it's so obvious. I can't believe I didn't see it before.

I think back to when Mum died. When Stella first came to me. Or I invented her. Whatever. It doesn't matter now. She showed up at school, in uniform. Yet she never took classes. Her name was never on the register.

And she waltzed into that game—Handstand Wonderland—the way I had wanted to for months, the way Mum had told me to, showing them that I was as good as they were. Better than them, because I practiced every afternoon after school against the barn. Every night against the bedroom wall. It was me the boys were watching, doing scissors and splits. No wonder Emily hated me. I took her place. Until Stella left and Emily was Queen Bee again.

Stella left. She left. But I don't know how. Or why. Maybe I had pills. Like Dad. Prozac or something. But I guess that's not the point. Because she came back. Because whatever drugs I take, she'll still be there, somewhere. Buried inside me. Forever.

Sometime around five I must have fallen asleep. It was getting light. I remember birds. Seagulls outside screeching their presence. I dreamed of horrible things. Babies with two heads. Siamese twins. A girl being sawn in two, each half a living thing on its own. B-movie schlock horror. Victorian freak-show stuff. I run to the bathroom. Morning sickness.

It's nine now. I can hear Dad and Alfie downstairs, Mrs. Hickman asking who used up the tea bags and telling Alfie to get some off the shelf. The sound of normal life. The sound of people who don't know there's a monster in the attic. Who think I've just had a row with my boyfriend, and it will all be all right in the morning. Well, it isn't.

I flush the toilet and look at myself in the mirror. Looking for signs of her. That she's in there somewhere. And there's nothing weird. No horns. No rolling eyes. But I can see what she's done to me, what I've done to myself, trying to be her. I touch my stomach again. And I know she hasn't gone. She is hiding, waiting.

I wash my face. I have work to do.

I sit at the computer, the door shut so I can flick to Facebook if someone comes in.

I don't know what I'm looking for. Anything, really.

Anything to tell me what I am. What to do. How to get rid of this feeling, this creature that is lurking in me, destroying me. I type in "imaginary friend," but I know she's not that. Imaginary friends are nice, aren't they? They come to tea. They play princesses, pirates, cowboys and Indians. And they don't come back when you're sixteen and sleep with your boyfriend.

I plow through studies, speculation. But nothing fits. How does it work? How does she do the bad stuff? How does she do things without me knowing? Then I remember. And I type in that line: "All the ways you wish you could be . . ."

There it is. The truth. She's not my fairy godmother. She's my wicked witch. My Tyler Durden. My alter ego.

There are pages and pages about it. Dissociative identity disorder, it's called. My ego, whatever that is, has disintegrated. Shocked by some event, some trauma, it has split in two.

And then it all clicks into place.

I see Mum that day. Mrs. Hickman picks me up from school, Dad still out in the fields checking the fences. And I run in, shouting her name, waving a picture I painted. But I trip over something in the living room. An arm. Her arm. At first I think it's a game. Sleeping lions. I laugh and tickle her. But she doesn't move. Then I see that her eyes are open, but glassy, lifeless. Blood trickles down from her mouth onto the rug. And then Mrs. Hickman is shouting at Ed to get out and pulling me away from the body. And I'm crying and clutching at her nightdress. Then I black out.

When I woke up, there were two of us. Jude, quiet, obliging. Who never fit in. Who never wore the right clothes or said the right thing. Who stayed on the edge of it all, hoping no one would notice her. Jude the Obscure.

And Stella, who wanted the world to look at her. Who spoke in practiced, scripted sound bites. Who wore clothes that said, "Look at me. Bright, shining Stella."

In a weird way, it makes sense, why that could happen. And I'm relieved there's a reason. But that's not enough, just knowing why. I need to know what to do now. How to go back, to before, when it was just me.

I keep reading, about time lapse now, a sort of memory loss. When specific blocks of time seem to have dropped out of your life. Or sometimes, you can feel like you've watched a film, when you've actually been part of it. The audition. Mr. Hughes. Blair.

I read that sometimes we're both there. We can talk to each other. And sometimes the stronger one — Stella — takes over. And I am just her.

Then I look for other people like me. But I just find lists of characters from books, films, TV shows. Jekyll and Hyde. That girl in *Heroes*. Some guy in an old American series called *Taxi*.

I click on Jekyll and Hyde, knowing it's fiction, but hoping there's an answer there somewhere. That Jekyll killed Hyde off somehow. But it turns out that Jekyll is weak. That his alter ego takes over, then kills them both. And I think of Stella taking over. Of me being swallowed by my bigger, brighter self.

I return to the list. Sméagol and Gollum. Stephen King's Odetta. That film *Identity*, where a guy on death row gets one of his alter egos to kill the others at a flood-bound motel. Nothing useful. Not unless I can get ahold of a knife or a secret potion. But I have nothing else to go on.

That afternoon I watch *Fight Club* again. Watch Jack's sneering revenge create mischief and mayhem. See him with a gun in his mouth. Urging Jack to kill them both. "We'll be legend," he says. "We won't grow old."

But I don't want to be legend. I want to live. I want to go to the Lab. It was me, me who passed the audition, me who is "touched." And I want Ed. And he wants me. I realize now why he hated Stella. Not because she was a bad influence, but because I was ill. He had to watch me suffer, be torn apart. So I can't tell him about this. Can't tell Dad either. Because if they know Stella is back, then they won't let me leave this place, this nonexistent life. And I will suffocate.

But I can't live with this creature, these creatures, inside me. Not just the baby. Her. My Gollum. My Hyde.

I have created a monster.

And now I have to destroy it.

26

I CLOSE one eye. Pull eyeliner across the rim. Sweeping it up. Like she does. "Live fast, die young, and leave a good-looking corpse," Stella always says. And I need to look the part. Need to look like I mean it. My hand is shaking, the line blurred. But I don't have time to wash it off. To start again.

I'm wearing the dress. The one I bought that first day in Dixie's. The one I wore that night at the Point. Converse on my feet now. Like Stella.

I choose a lipstick. Red. The reddest I can find. Mascara. And perfume. Chanel No. 5.

Done, I stare at my reflection for one last time. Remembering what I look like, in case I never see it again.

At least like this. I am tired, bruised circles under my eyes, but beautiful still. In my own way. I see that now. I see her in me. Mum. Her eyes, her smile. And it's nice to know that part of me is a bit like her.

I don't write a note. Because I'm not killing myself. What would I say, anyway? The usual teen blah about darkness and tormented souls and half-lives? Or that I'm too fat, or ugly? Or that Marilyn Manson made me do it? I don't feel that. I want to live. I do. But if I'm going to live, I need to do it without her.

I go downstairs. Alfie is watching some wildlife program on TV. A polar bear killing a seal, its blood staining the snow.

He looks up. "Jude, did you know that polar bear liver is poisonous? It's because of vitamin A. If you ate one, you'd die."

It is seven o'clock. Dad has gone out. Some post office thing. I am supposed to be babysitting.

I switch the telly off.

"I was watching that."

"We're going out."

"Where?" Alfie is suspicious. Knows I have been told to stay in.

"Mrs. Hickman's," I say. "Get a toothbrush. And pajamas or something."

Alfie is full of questions. "Is it a sleepover? Are we going to watch films? Will Ed be there? Can I sleep in the same room as you?"

"Yes. No. I don't know. Maybe."

"What about Dad?"

"I'll leave him a note."

And I do. While Alfie packs for his adventure, I scrawl a message on the back of a receipt. My last words, after all. "Gone out. Alfie at Ed's." I add an x. Just in case.

Alfie and I walk up the hill. I can feel him looking at me. At my dress. The makeup.

"Are you going to a party?" he asks. "With Ed?"

"No," I say. "Not a party. Not with Ed."

He thinks for a moment. "With Stella?"

It is strange to hear the name out loud. I nod.

"Will you come back?"

He means tonight. But in my head I hear "ever."

I cross my fingers behind my back. "Yes."

As we reach the church, I can see the Land Rover parked on the curb. Ed is back.

I knock at the door. See the light of the telly flicker behind the curtains. *EastEnders*. Her not-so-secret addiction.

Mrs. Hickman answers.

"Hi," I say, smiling. Like the Jehovahs. Selling happiness in the form of a nine-year-old.

She is not buying it. "Aren't you s'posed to be babysitting?"

"Well, I am. But I need to do something. And I wouldn't normally ask, but he's been dying to come over."

Alfie is peering inside. "Can I watch telly?"

Mrs. Hickman is won over. "'Course. Go on in, love. There's biscuits on the table."

But I don't get away so easily.

"Where are you going, Jude?"

I don't have an answer. But then Ed is at her shoulder, saying it's all right, he'll sort it out.

She looks at me. At my breasts half showing, at the lipstick, my hair. Worried. For me, for Ed. But she goes in. To give Alfie milk and cookies. Mum things. And we are left there, inches apart, a gulf between us.

My stomach fills with butterflies again. Not because of what I'm about to do, but because it means we will never be the same. Everything will be different from now on.

I am the first to speak.

"You're back." It's obvious. Facile. I cringe.

He nods.

"Was it good?"

"I guess."

I asked for this. I know. The short answers. The shrugs. But it hurts.

"Ed—"

"So, where *are* you going?"

"I can't . . ." I trail off. There is so much I want to tell him. About me. About her. That I love him. That I always have, and I always will. But I don't have time. Just enough for two words.

"I'm sorry." And then I kiss him. Hard. With all the love I felt that first time, all the love I feel now that has built up over the years.

He pulls away. "Jude—"

"Don't say anything." I don't want to hear it. I know he is scared now. So I kiss him again. And as his eyes close and his lips touch mine, I reach out to a hook behind the door and slip the Land Rover keys into my pocket.

He watches me from the doorstep walking slowly up the road. I don't look back. Just listen for the familiar thud of the door closing.

When it does, I stop. Wait. Sit in the bus shelter, amid the candy wrappers and smell of pee, watching the thunder clouds gather and the rain start to fall.

Ten minutes later, I run back down the road, keys damp in my palm. Rain soaking me in seconds, slicking my hair to my face like seaweed. I turn the key and the door opens with a clunk, like the volume has been turned up. I don't move. Worried he will have heard it and come running. Stop me.

But he doesn't. The rain drowns out the sound. Like it's been turned on for me. For this night.

I climb in, pull the door in gently. Will slam it later when I'm out of earshot. I look at the dashboard. It is years since I drove. Since Dad taught me to steer the tractors, letting me change gear. Then Ed showing me how to drive the Land Rover. Us bouncing up and down the dirt roads, shrieking with laughter, stalling it, nearly backing into the barn.

I slot the key into the ignition. Pray that it will start the first time instead of its usual coughing diesel splutter. And I am stunned when it does, just slips into life. Without looking up at the house, I slam it into first and let the brake off. Right foot on the accelerator, left foot hard down on the clutch, raising it to find the biting point. But my foot, wet with rain, slips. It revs, metal screeching, and stalls.

I can see Mrs. Penleaze coming down the road. Frowning at the stranger behind the wheel.

"Come on," I say out loud. I turn it off and on again. Into gear. Raise the clutch, depress the accelerator. And it moves.

I put my foot down, flooding the engine with petrol, putting it into second. Find the windshield wipers. I'm gone.

I drive up past the houses, then turn left onto the coast road. To where I know she will find me. To where she will leave me at last.

I am in front of the fence. Facing the sea. Roaring. Tide swelling in the storm. Rain hammering the windshield. And into the noise I scream.

"Stella . . . come on . . . I'm here . . . There's no me without you."

And I keep on screaming until she comes.

27

SHE SITS in the passenger seat, smoking.

She looks stunning. Wearing one of Mum's dresses, all corset and black satin. Heels to match. Hair up. Eighties coke whore.

"Bloody rain. My hair's a mess." She fiddles with a strand in the mirror. Then drops it.

"You look beautiful," I say.

She turns toward me. "You too."

I smile and look at my reflection in the rearview mirror. My hair bottle-bleached and salt-dirty, my eyes ringed in black, lips stained red. My hands on the steering wheel, knuckles white, the nail varnish chipped, weeks old. Then I look at the Point, falling away in front of us. The wooden fence, broken from where we've climbed over it so many times. The ledge below, cigarette-strewn and soaked in lager. And the sea below that. A swirling, monstrous, beautiful thing. Alive.

Nausea rises in me again, bubbling up, insistent. I breathe in, pushing it, willing it back down again. I don't know how we got here. How I got here. I don't mean how I got to this place, the Point, but how I became the girl in the mirror. I don't recognize myself. What I look like. What I'm doing.

I used to know who I was. Jude. Named after a song in the hope that I'd stand out and shine. But I didn't. Jude the Invisible. Jude the Obscure. Everything about me unremarkable. Nothing beautiful or striking, to make people say, "You know, the girl with that hair," or those eyes. I was just the girl from the farm. The one with no mum. I knew what would happen when I woke up, when I went to school, when I came home. Who would talk to me. Who wouldn't.

Until Stella. Now when I look in the mirror, I see someone else staring back. I can't see where I stop and Stella begins.

"We'll be legend," I say.

I watch Stella as she lights up a cigarette and drops the Zippo on the dash.

"Like Thelma and Louise," she drawls. She takes a drag then passes it to me. "But without the head scarves or Brad Pitt or the heart-of-gold cop watching us die."

And then I know she knows. And I know she won't stop me. Because this is the only way.

"It'll be very," she says.

I take a long drag on the cigarette and, still watching myself in the mirror, exhale slowly. *Shouldn't be smoking,* I think. But what difference does it make now? I pass it back to Stella. Then I let the hand brake off and the car rolls forward. I feel it hit the fence, hear the wood cracking beneath us. The car jerks down over the rock. We are at the top ledge now.

Stella shrieks. Fear? No, delight. Even in death she wants to stand out, shine. She takes my hand. And I am holding part of me. A part that I had longed for. Had begged to return. Like some boy who is beautiful under the strobes and half light of a club, when you're drowned in vodka or Pernod. But then you see him in the harsh unforgiving light of day, and you realize that you never wanted it at all.

And so I do it. My one hope of losing her and keeping me. I snatch my hand from her grasp and click open my seat belt. "I'm sorry," I cry as the car pitches forward. And then it's like some disaster movie. Fast and slow at the same time. I pull the door handle, desperately pushing against its weight with my shoulder. Stella reaches out and tries to hold me back. My arm flails out and hits her full on the cheek. I feel the pain sear through me. But she doesn't flinch, just grasps my arm. And I think, *I have lost. This is it. It's over.* But suddenly I feel other hands, stronger hands, gripping me hard. Pulling me out. Away from her. I jump.

For a brief moment, I am in two places.

I feel my body smack the ground, the crack of my leg breaking beneath me, my skull hitting a rock.

And I feel Stella flung forward into the windshield. Hear the suck as the sea floods in through the cracked glass. The muffled echoey sound of her pulse as her head goes under. The gurgle as she opens her mouth to breathe and water rushes into her throat and lungs.

Then I'm in his arms. My body broken, his head on my chest, the tears mixing with the rain and the blood. Then everything goes black. There is no sound. It is over. She is gone. The curtain falls.

28

I WAKE up in the hospital, three days later. Alfie sitting next to me, dressed as a crocodile again, reading *Hello!* Dad silent, clutching his hands so tight that I can see his knuckles whiten.

"Hi." My voice is croaky. Every inch of me hurts. My head, my leg, my stomach.

"Jude. Oh, my God." Dad reaches forward and presses a button, and nurses flood in. Like angels in blue and white. I pass out again.

The doctors say I'm lucky. I guess I am. Lucky that Alfie told Ed about Stella. Lucky that Ed knew where I would go. That he ran to Matt's and got his camper van in time to reach me, to pull me out before the Land Rover took me down with it. Lucky he'd called the coast guard and the helicopter was airborne before I'd even reached the Point. Lucky my broken ribs didn't puncture my lung. And that I blacked out before the pain made me panic and lose too much blood.

Or maybe luck doesn't come into it. Maybe my fairy godmother was looking out for me after all.

I come home. Dad shows me the clippings from the paper. The wreckage. Then photos from the hospital. My own face, battered and bloated in purple, red, and black. And I cry. Every day I cry. Because of what I've done. And what I've lost. Because I am alive.

And I am alive. My legs still in casts. Taking morphine three times a day. And other drugs too. No chance of starting at the Lab this year. But they've held my place. And Ed's at King's. He's deferring, going to work on the boats for a year, earn some money. Then away in Matt's camper for a bit. I'm going with him. Dad says it will be good for me. To get away. I said he should think about it himself, getting away. From here. From her. The memories. He smiled, said, "Maybe." But I know he won't.

I never told Blair. Never spoke to him about that night. But it's over now, the baby gone. I've asked Ed how he feels, knowing he wasn't the first. But he says it doesn't matter. And I believe him. Because that wasn't me.

I was someone else then. Someone I thought I wanted to be. Someone for whom the world would spin alone. Someone who took dares, picked fights, smoked, drank, danced in high heels above the sea.

Now I'm just Jude.